THE

ARENA

THE ADVENTURES OF HORC:

BOOK 2

BY DREW SEREN

See what Drew Seren is up to.
Visit his website www.drewseren.com
And sign up for his newsletter

Copyright 2018 © MysticHawker Press
http://www.mystichawker.com/

ISBN: 978-1-945632-35-8

Edited by Robert Brownson
Cover design by Anadia-chan
www.anadia-chan.com

1

THE BRIGHT sun blazed down as Horc and his party trudged across the Scalteon Desert. For a couple of hours, they'd walked along the packed dirt road with very little distinction from the rolling white sand that made up the desert dunes. Horc never imagined he'd be able to sweat in a game, but that's what he was doing as he stared across the bleak landscape. He wanted to stop somewhere in the shade and take a nap, but there was no shade; there was just the seemingly never-ending rise and fall of the sand dunes.

"Okay, this is really getting monotonous," Steelmaiden, the large Barbarian woman next to him, said. "I can't wait until we can get mounts. Does anyone know what level that is?"

"Let me check and see if anyone's reached it yet," Slasher, their Fighter, said.

"The way our luck is going, probably not," Horc mumbled. Although he'd been having a lot of fun in the game, long times of travel made him tired and frustrated. They gave him time to think about how his body was trapped in his gaming pod in his basement after a tornado wiped out his house and neighborhood. From the last report he received from one of the game admins, the rescue team had reached his house, but were having to proceed very carefully to excavate things in hopes of getting him out alive. As he traversed dune after dune with his wolf companion, and his party members at his side, his mind kept going back to how close to death he was. He felt fine in the game of Halfworld, but if his pod malfunctioned further than it had already, or something heavy managed to break through the titanium steel casing, he was going to be a goner.

"Looks like level thirty," Slasher said. "Someone from the Berlin office posted in the Wiki a little while ago that they'd managed to get a mount and it was really making getting around a lot easier."

Horc let out a long heavy sigh. "So, ten more levels. Since each level takes more to complete than the previous one, that's going to take a while." He reached down and scratched his wolf's ears, wishing his wolf was big enough he could ride it and stop some of the pain in his feet.

"It's all part of the game," Steelmaiden said. "Although I was hoping for level twenty-five, since it didn't happen at level twenty. I guess we should be trying to kill everything that'll get us points, but not kill us first."

"I think, if anything happens to Horc, Greensleeves and Baladara will kill us," Slasher said.

"Then we pick our targets carefully," Steelmaiden replied. "It's not like there's much out here in this desert besides snakes, scorpions, vultures, and tortoises."

"Right," Slasher agreed. "But that last pair of vultures nearly took you out, remember. Without our healer, we've got to be careful."

Steelmaiden frowned but didn't say anything.

Horc stayed quiet too. It felt weird playing the game, actually going to a new area without Baladara and Greensleeves, who'd been with him since the beginning of the game. But Baladara, the party mage, was the only member of their group who wasn't using a game pod, just VR goggles and gloves. In real life, his body got tired from hours of game play. He declared himself in need of a little rest.

Greensleeves, their druid and healer, had logged out to see if there was something any of them could do to help cover Horc during his time in Red Wind Terrace. The Orc starting city wasn't exactly friendly to humans unless the players worked on building their reputation with the Orcs. Since none of their party, other than Horc, had any reputation with the Orcs, they would have to wait outside the city for Horc unless they could find a neutral area for them to relax in while Horc went to complete his quest. Horc only had a neutral rep with the Orcs due to him being a Half Orc. If he'd been full Orc, he'd be in good standing with the Orcs as opposed to neutral.

"Maybe there's just one of those guys." Steelmaiden unsheathed her massive sword and pointed up the dune to the white scorpion that was a shade off from the color of the sand and the size of a Mini Cooper that was starting down toward them.

Sandslasher, level 21, proclaimed the red text above the scorpion.

"Maybe." Horc pulled out his bow and strung an Impact Arrow.

"Bring it down," Slasher said as he stepped up next to Steelmaiden, his own sword bare and ready to swing.

Adding a Flaming Arrow spell to the Impact Arrow to do more damage, Horc let his arrow fly at the Sandslasher. It hit and knocked about a quarter of the creature's health bar down.

The scorpion hissed and rushed toward them, kicking up a cloud of white sand in its wake. It moved so fast that Horc wondered how fast it could've moved without the Impact Arrow slowing its movements.

Horc got off another shot, a Razor Arrow with a Poison Dart spell on it. The damage wasn't as much, but the scorpion was within range of Steelmaiden, the wolf, and Slasher. It only took a couple more rounds of attacks to bring the Sandslasher down. As soon as Slasher finished looting it, Horc skinned it. It blinked and faded from existence seconds after Horc pulled the tough but valuable shell from it.

"You know, we're going to need to get into a town soon," Slasher said. "My bags are about full, and I think you two aren't much better off."

Horc pulled up his inventory and frowned. "Four slots for me."

"Six for me," Steelmaiden said. "Another drawback to missing the rest of the party, we can't pass things around to get nice stacks. Not that a ton of the stuff we've gotten stacks right anyway. So many different critters, so many different drops." She pulled a rag and wiped her sword free of bug guts before sheathing it. "And it wasn't even worth that much as far as XP goes. I'm still a long way from not having to walk everywhere."

Closing his inventory screen, Horc shouldered his bow. At least he wasn't having to worry about arrows anymore, not after finding the Everfull Quiver in the Gnoll King's Dungeon. But he still had bag-space issues. They'd all emptied as much as they could before they set out. It was obvious, from looking at the maps of the area, that it would take them a while to get there, and the odds were that they'd run into a few mobs along the way. The maps had been accurate, and with the drops from the mobs, they were quickly running low on space.

Steelmaiden got a faraway look, something that was indicative of her either checking her wiki, or maps. The game wiki was quickly adding entries as more and more players explored the world, but there was still a lot to do to get it up to the level of being extremely useful when players got stuck on what to do next. After a moment, Steelmaiden blinked. "Okay, that might be a good option."

"What?" Horc asked as he pulled a chunk of meat out for his wolf. After every fight, he tried to give his companion a little something, just to make sure his health was maxed out in case they ran into trouble.

"There's a small village not far from here." Steelmaiden pointed to their north across the dune the scorpion had come from. "According to the map, it's a yellow village for me, so it's neutral. We're about an hour or so from Red Wind Terrace. Maybe Slasher and I can stay there while you go complete your quest. We might even be able to pick up some quests that'll help with our reputation among the Orcs, since we're on the edge of their controlled zone."

Slasher nodded as he sheathed his sword. "That makes sense. If we can up our rep with them, we'll be able to enter their city, so we don't have to break up the party."

"Except for the asshole players who haven't adapted to the idea that this game is reputation-based and not totally faction-based," Horc said, remembering how some of the human players in Stone Helm City reacted to a Half Orc wandering around in the human starting zone. Although the NPCs hadn't had an issue with it as long as his rep with the humans remained decent, he'd had a couple of challenges to his right to be there by overzealous players.

"There will always be those," Slasher said. "And if we're in a party, we'll be better equipped to handle them."

Steelmaiden nodded. "He's got a point. So, let's head over to Tragiczan and settle in there while you head on to Red Wind and hopefully by the time you're done there, the others will be with us."

"Okay." Horc looked up the dune the scorpion had come over and hoped there wasn't a nest full of them on the other side. Even staying on the road hadn't stopped them from running into mobs. He was fairly sure getting off the road and going cross country was going to be even more of a challenge. At least they hadn't run into anything they couldn't handle.

2

"THAT'S IT, I'm full." Horc closed his inventory screen after pulling in the last hide he had skinned from yet another Sandslasher.

"Me too," Steelmaiden agreed. "But I think Tragiczan should be just over this dune. If the map's accurate."

Slasher made it to the top of the dune and looked back over his shoulder. "We've got a town down there."

A wave of fatigue washed over Horc. "Let's get down there and empty these bags out and get off our feet for a little while."

Steelmaiden headed up the dune first. "Sounds good to me."

Horc hurried to follow with his wolf companion at his heels. He was incredibly tired of wading through the deep sand that made up the dunes and often spilled over onto the roads and paths that crisscrossed the desert. He felt like he had sand in everything he was wearing with at least two inches filling his boots and socks. Since he hadn't taken time to look at the map, he had no clue if there was a road between Tragiczan and Red Wind Terrace. He hoped there was, as it would make the going a lot easier, both in terms of avoiding some mobs, and the sand that seemed like the prevailing element in the desert they'd trooped through.

From the top of the dune, the village of Tragiczan was visible. A series of large tents spread around a central square that looked to be of a similar packed-earth creation as the road they'd been on for hours. The tents were mostly bright colors, some dulled by obvious exposure to the wind and sand. There were two black tents at the farthest point from the dune they were walking down.

"What's with the black tents?" Horc asked as the warm wind picked up and blew even more sand into his clothing and face.

"We'll have to check them out when we get there," Steelmaiden said. "In a lot of games, something like black tents means trouble."

"Maybe it's how the town got its name," Slasher added. "The black tents bring something tragic with them."

Horc wasn't in the mood for something tragic. He wanted to empty his bags and get off his feet for a few minutes before continuing on with just his wolf at his side.

A large burly man with short tusks sticking out of human lips, and white hair poking from under his helmet stepped in front of them as they neared the edge of the village. "Hold." His voice was human, but his skin had a faint green shading to it and he was broader than even the guards at Stone Helm City. His armor was leather, and well scarred, and he held a huge, wicked-looking spear. The yellow lettering over his head declared him to be **Tragiczan Guard, level XXX.**

Steelmaiden stopped in front of him. "Is there a problem? We're just travelers looking for an escape from the desert." Her tone was soft, and her posture the least aggressive Horc had ever seen.

"We don't want any trouble here," the guard said. "We're neutral. That means no fighting among Humans and Orcs. If you start any problems, they and you will be dealt with. Is that clear?"

Steelmaiden smiled at him. "Of course. We'll be good. Do we look like the types who would cause trouble?"

The guard studied them for a moment, then shook his head. "A Ranger, a Barbarian, and a Fighter. Not a really diverse party. No real blemishes on any of your reputations. Okay. But I'm serious, start any trouble and you're out of here. I don't care if there's a sandstorm going on, you'll be out of my hair faster than a viper can hit a hare."

"Thanks." Steelmaiden flashed him another smile and they moved on past. "They might be neutral, but they're serious about their security."

"Probably have to be," Slasher said. "They're on the border of Orc territory. That could be rather dicey at times, I bet."

"Depends on what the AI does with it, or what kind of sods the players are wanting to be." Steelmaiden angled them over toward a tent that had several tables full of wares set up along its shaded edge.

A tall Orc woman leaned over the table as they approached. "Adventurers, come, come, see what I have to offer." The yellow text above her head read **Asheena, Merchant, Level XXX**.

Seeing the way the woman's low-cut tunic barely contained her immense bosom, Horc bit back a laugh. The XXX had too many connotations in that moment.

"I think we're more interested in selling," Steelmaiden rested an elbow on the table, obviously careful of the ends of several wicked-looking swords. "But if you've got anything I like the looks of." There was a slightly flirty tone to her words.

Asheena smiled. "I always like buying from experienced adventurers such as yourselves. Come, let me see what you have, and see what bargains we can make."

They haggled for a good half an hour over everything in their inventories they wanted to sell and over a massive long sword Asheena had that Steelmaiden liked the looks of. In the end, Horc walked away from the tent with his coin pouch several gold heavier. Steelmaiden didn't make as much money, but she had the new sword strapped to her back and a swagger in her step. Slasher came out ahead with some stronger armor, even if it did have a badly repaired dent on one shoulder. Asheena was also nice enough to point them toward the blacksmith a couple of tents away for armor and weapon repairs, which they were all in need of after their trip across the desert.

Two hours later, they made it to the small inn, that was actually underground. The place had a front that resembled a tent, but there were instantly steps going down a good floor and a half underground. The air there was a lot cooler than what Horc was slowly becoming accustomed to in their journey across the blazing parched landscape they'd been traveling through.

"You know, we still don't know why they call this place Tragiczan," Slasher said as they walked down the narrow hallway to the room he and Steelmaiden were going to share for a day or so while Horc went to the Orc starting city.

Steelmaiden shrugged. "Hard to tell, really. It might just be somewhat of a joke with the developers, or there might be some tale we can learn as we talk with the local NPCs. While Horc's away, we can do some digging and see what we can come up with."

Slasher opened the door to their room. "Sounds like a way to keep things from getting too boring."

"And we don't want you two to get bored," Horc said as he followed the others in. "You know, if you need to, you could just log out for a little while."

"Nope." Steelmaiden shook her head and she flopped on the closest bed. "Not going to do that. We promised the others we were going to look after you while they were gone, and that's what we're going to do. My pod's working right, or I would've had an error pop up, so I'm in this for the long haul."

Horc didn't doubt her, but he was getting tired of his friends watching over him like a bunch of mother hens. He was looking forward to getting away from them for a little while and seeing what was waiting for him in Red Wind Terrace. Sure, there was a good chance that if he died in game, he might die in real life. But they didn't know for sure. They had no way to know until something happened. With his pod buried under the remains of his house and his log-out button grayed out, nobody knew exactly what was going on. The fact that the game was still in beta-testing didn't help. The documentation was minimal, but what Horc did know was he wasn't going to sit around and 'stay safe' the way the game admins wanted him to.

"She's right." Slasher patted the other bed and causing a small cloud of dust to roll up around his hand. He frowned. "Besides, we might figure out some things about the game, and we can spend a little time updating the wiki. Remember that message we all got through the system a little while ago about the added bonus for every addition to the wiki we make. Gives us all an excellent opportunity for more real money from playing."

"I bet they're getting complaints about the wiki being all-but useless," Steelmaiden said as she got off the bed and dusted herself off. "You know, sometimes this game is just a little too real, but I guess that's not a bad thing. But if they included bedbugs, I'm going to be pissed. That might require me at least talking to Greensleeves's husband. There's no point in going that far with virtual reality."

Horc chuckled. After what they'd endured with actually sweating in a game, he was a little surprised she was complaining about bugs, but he wouldn't be surprised if the game designers had thought of that too. "Well, if you two are satisfied with the room, why don't we go eat, and then I'll head on to Red Wind Terrace?"

"Sounds good," Steelmaiden agreed. "And we'll make sure to keep in touch if any of us find out anything interesting."

"Yeah." Horc head for the door. "I'd still like to know why this place is called Tragiczan."

"Me too. Honestly, it's a little creepy." Steelmaiden followed him out into the hallway.

"Some designer was probably just having fun with it," Slasher said as he locked the door back and pocketed the key. "These guys have warped senses of humor."

"Yeah, they do," Horc agreed. Although he hadn't seen much of it in Halfworld yet, there were always some kind of odd or hidden meanings behind a lot of the things that happened in games. It was funny enough that all the bosses in the Gnoll King's dungeon looked like various managers from their company, Total Immersion Systems, he figured there were bound to be more. For all they knew, the mayor or chief of Tragiczan was modeled after an ex of one of the designers and it was just an inside joke.

WHEN HORC settled into his chair on the main floor of the inn, his axe bumped against his back. He reached back and shifted it slightly to a more comfortable position, so the blade wasn't pressing against his spine. "You know, I can't decide if I want to get rid of this thing or not."

Steelmaiden cocked her head. "What thing?"

"This axe. I mean it still has a decent attack, but since Miranda took out the Gnoll King, all I can get it to do is look cheap. Before that it was throwing different power blasts each time I hit one of the crystals. Now… nothing." He'd really hoped that, after a cool down, each of the crystals would get a charge again, but that hadn't happened. It was like it only had magic inside the dungeon.

"Let me see." Steelmaiden reached across the table for the big axe.

Horc pulled it off his shoulder and passed it to her.

She took it and looked closely at the gems set in its handle. She rolled it around in her hand, frowning.

The bar maid, another buxom Orc woman came over and took their orders, then hurried back to the bar area.

"Looks like the magic has been drained out of it," Steelmaiden said. "I can't be sure, but from other games I've played, that looks like what's happened. Maybe you can find an enchanter to put charges back into the stones." She handed the axe back across the table to Horc.

Frowning, Horc put the axe back across his shoulder, careful to position the blade so it wasn't doing any damage to himself. "Why do I think that's going to be expensive?"

"Probably because it is, unless we happen to find an enchanter who's looking for a party and would be willing to trade services, or something," Slasher said.

"And an enchanter is a class?" Horc leaned on the table, putting his chin in his hands.

Slasher shook his head. "Nope, it's one of the professions, like skinning."

"One plus to that is you could request certain spells be laid on the crystals," Steelmaiden suggested as the barmaid returned with their drinks.

"So, if I didn't like the cold blast the axe gave off, I could switch that out for a flaming blade or something?" Horc lifted his pewter tankard and took a sip of the ale. It was some of the best he'd ever tasted, not that he spent tons of time tasting beer, but he did drink from time to time, and the one he was drinking in game beat out any of the light beers he normally had.

Steelmaiden nodded slightly as she took a sip of her beer. She wiped some of the foam off her lips with the back of her sleeve. "Exactly. But it all depends on what the enchanter you find has available. While you're in Red Wind Terrace, you might check around and see who you can find there. Check prices. Or you might wait until Baladara gets back and hits her level twenty when we get the second profession slot."

"Okay. Yeah. That reminds me, I need to think about what other profession I want to take, don't I? There should be a trainer of just about anything in a starting city." Horc took another drink of the beer. It gave him a sense of vitality, without any of the mental clouding he was used to hearing about with beer.

"Right. We all need to think about that. If we're going to stay a party after we get you out of the pod, we might start to think about complementary professions," Slasher said. "Right now, we're doing okay, although I think either Steelmaiden or myself should take some kind of prospecting or mineral craft, I haven't checked to see what they call it here, but that way the others can get blacksmithing, or weaponry skills and handle all our repairs." He touched the dent that was still slightly visible on his new breastplate, even after they stopped at the local blacksmith, and frowned. "We'd have to be better than some of the things we've run into so far."

"We'll talk about it." Steelmaiden flashed him a wicked grin. "For now, we'll do some poking about town and see what we can find. I hope there's a Barbarian trainer. I could use a few things since we went up on the road here."

Horc finished off his beer. "Good, then sounds like we all have plans. I don't know how long I'll be in Red Wind Terrace, but I'll keep you guys up to date, and if they send me on any quests outside the immediate Orc area, I'll let you know."

"And we'll also see if we can get some quests around here to help with our Orc reputation," Steelmaiden said.

As Horc stood and started toward the door with his wolf at his side, he felt strange. As much as he wanted his new friends to stop fussing over him, there was an odd sense of leaving them alone as he headed off to somewhere they couldn't go with him. He hoped everyone was going to be okay until they got back together.

3

A ROUGH stone pillar served as a sign post pointing Horc up a trail toward a deep canyon in the desert. He wasn't sure how long he'd been walking since leaving Tragiczan. Luckily, there had been a narrow trail of a road that led from the village to the main road running toward Red Wind Terrace. It provided him with a fairly safe route to take. The one scorpion he'd encountered had been a level 20 and had gone down fairly quick between his arrows and his wolf's fangs and claws.

The sun was starting down toward the western horizon. It made him wonder how the rescuers were coming in getting the debris of his house clear, so they could reach his pod. He'd been in the game for over two days, going on three IRL. Nobody had really said if the game was synched with regular time or not, but he presumed it was. Most of the games he'd played had run on a similar clock, except for a few of the larger, slower planets he visited in Galactic Explorers.

The road dropped off as he came around a bend and the red rocks of the canyon walls spread out before him. The walls were fifty or sixty feet deep and lined with terraces. It reminded Horc of some ancient Native American cliff dwellings he'd visited on a summer vacation in Colorado when he'd been in high school. He was so far away he couldn't make out details of the people moving around on the sandstone ledges, but there seemed to be a ton of them. The road ran straight down, heading toward the heart of the canyon. A number of buildings sat on the canyon floor, although at the distance

Horc was from them, it was difficult to tell much in the way of size. They looked more like boulders than buildings. The only thing that made him think they were buildings was the number of people who seemed to be going into the dark spots on them, which he presumed were doors, or doorways.

"Looks like we found the place," Horc muttered, and at his side, his wolf whined softly. From the first step on his companion quests he'd been surprised by how real the companion animals were in game. His wolf acted more like a huge lanky dog than how he expected a wolf to act. When he got out of the game—*if* he got out—he was going to have to congratulate the designers and let them know they'd accomplished something phenomenal with the details they'd programed into Halfworld.

About halfway down the canyon, the walls narrowed, blocking part of his view of the city. Huge wood and iron gates stood open but looked like they could be closed at a moment's notice by the two hulking Orcs on either side of them. The Orc guards were in heavy chainmail armor, and each carried a huge axe that looked like it could cleave Horc in half if it barely tapped him. There was a decidedly dangerous glint in their beady red eyes.

The guard on the left glanced at the one on the right who gave an almost imperceptible nod. If Horc hadn't been watching them so closely as he approached, he'd have missed it. Left guard sighed, straightened slightly, and trudged toward Horc, his heavy leather boots kicking up small clouds of dust with each step he took.

When he was a couple of feet from Horc, his text was visible. **Red Wind Terrace Guard, Level XXX**. The triple x didn't feel funny—it felt extreme.

"What's your business?" the guard grumbled.

"Got a quest to see Ranger Thunderbow." Horc carefully didn't look at the guard's face. He didn't want to do anything that might antagonize the big Orc.

"Fairly neutral." The guard nodded slowly. "I guess it's okay to let you in. Sometimes you halflings cause problems. Don't ever forget that we have tons of guards here in Red Wind Terrace. You start anything—we'll be all over you like flies on shit. You'll lose most of your good rep with us and we'll kick you out into the sand. You and your little wolf too."

Horc nodded, not wanting to do anything to cause problems for either him or his companion. "I got it."

"Good. Now do you know where to find Thunderbow?" The guard looked down his prominent green nose that nearly brushed his long white tusks. "I mean, if you got a quest, you should know where to find him."

Pulling up his map, the yellow dot for Thunderbow was much deeper into the city. There was something next to it that said 'L2'. "Yeah… I guess the L2 means level two."

"Exactly. You can take any of the lifts, but the first one will probably get you there faster." The guard pointed to the right, toward something on the other side of the heavy doors, something Horc couldn't see.

"Thanks." Horc waited until the guard took a couple of steps back toward his post on the left side of the door, then hurried past. The Orc guards were definitely a lot rougher around the edges than the human guards in Stone Helm City had been. But it was a different culture, so Horc wasn't surprised.

Right after the gate, the road opened up and split into three parts, one heading along each side of the canyon, and one going up the middle. Orcs and many other races wandered around the area. There were a lot more races in Red Wind Terrace than there had been in

Stone Helm City. Horc recognized Orcs, and Half Orcs, although the Half Orcs seemed to have a large spectrum of skin tinting, ranging from a pale, almost pastel shade to a deep forest. He hadn't bothered to go through everything when he was designing his toon, so he was surprised by the variations he saw on the street. The Orcs themselves had a lot of difference in skin tones but it seemed that they never got as dark or as light as the Half Orcs. There were also Elves, but they looked different than Baladara's classic blonde hair, blue eyed, frail creature. Some had dark hair, eyes, and skin—others were shades of brown, looking more buff than Baladara could ever look. There were also several more animalistic races that Horc didn't really want to stare at too long trying to figure out what they were supposed to be.

He found a lift, which was basically an open-air platform that went up and down along the side of the cliff dwellings. Horc wasn't sure it was particularly safe. After watching it go up and down with short stops on each level, Horc figured that it wasn't completely safe, but he knew how it worked and hoped that neither he nor the wolf would off-balance the thing and cause them all to plummet to their deaths.

Swallowing back a wave of fear that left his hands sweaty, Horc forced himself to step onto the wooden platform that was being lifted up the side of the cliff by a chain that disappeared at the top of the canyon wall.

"Hey hold up," a light brown elf player shouted, running toward the lift. The text above his head was green and read **Greensleeves, Sand Elf, Druid, Level 21.**

Horc stared at him. He didn't know there could be two players with the same name. It must be a bug in the system. "Sorry, can't stop it," he called back.

"Wait when you get off," Greensleeves said, sounding familiar.

"David?" Horc stared down at the man waiting for the lift to return. How had he managed to change races and still keep his level? He hadn't had time to get a new toon up that high, had he? Did Halfworld even allow people to have multiple toons? He hadn't bothered to check any of that when he'd created Horc, he'd just done everything random and taken what the system had given him.

"Yeah. Stay there." Greensleeves held up a hand for him to stay put as he got off the lift at the second level.

Horc got off the lift when it stopped and his wolf followed him. There wasn't anyone at that level trying to get on, so he stood there and waited. Farther down the terrace, people came out of the buildings, which being closer were obviously shops, based on the signs hanging over their doors. Horc didn't know what some of the symbols on the signs meant, but from the crossed axes on one, he presumed it was a weapons vendor.

The lift finished going up to the next level above him and started down. A small green man with big pointed ears ran past Horc. "If you're not getting on, I will. It's rude to just stand there and block the way."

"Sorry." Horc took a step back toward the nearest building, one that had a sign with a couple of sheaves of grain that might be a baker. Seconds later the little man disappeared as the lift dropped below the second-tier floor.

Horc took a deep breath and caught the smell of freshly baked bread, reinforcing the idea that the store he stood next to was a bakery. He wondered if the bread would taste as good as it smelled. So far, everything he'd eaten or drunk on Halfworld had tasted awesome.

"Why does everyone around here stand by the lifts?" The little green man's voice carried from the first floor. "Geez, you guys need to learn some manners."

About a minute later, Greensleeves appeared as the lift carried him up to Horc's level. He was a lot different from his human form. He was shorter, more willowy. His skin was a soft brown and his hair and round eyes were dark brown. "So, what do you think?" He wore loose leather armor that was a soft beige that reminded Horc of the Sandslasher scorpions near Tragiczan. It looked like he was outfitted to blend into the desert.

"How'd you change races?" Horc stopped staring at his friend.

"Had Rick do some game designer magic. After Baladara said she'd gotten a guard to send her to the human-starting city, I got to thinking. While I was logged out, Rick and I talked it over." He pointed down the terrace, indicating for Horc to start walking.

Not wanting to have another toon go off on him for standing around, Horc complied.

"I thought about either turning into an Orc or a Half Orc, since that would help me stay with you and keep you safe," Greensleeves continued as they walked.

"You guys do know I really don't need babysitters," Horc said, trying hard to keep the irritation he felt at his friends doing their best to make sure he stayed safe. He didn't want them to think he needed their overprotectiveness, but it was nice to have.

Greensleeves nodded. "I do. But since we're doing the whole party thing, having members of our group with you makes things easier. I noticed you left Steelmaiden and Slasher in Tragiczan. Right?"

"Right. They're going to try to get some quests that'll help bring their reputation with the Orcs high enough they can come to Red Wind Terrace, or wherever my quests take me."

"And since you're neutral, there might be places we can't go unless we're neutral too," Greensleeves continued. "I've always liked playing elves, and if Rick hadn't been so adamant about me going through the Gnoll King's Dungeon, I'd have gone Elf when I started. But I'm glad I didn't, since you guys are cool and I like running with you. But Rick and I went over the various races—there are a fair number that start out neutral, even a couple of elves. Then we had to go over the various class limitations. That was one of the reasons I didn't want to go Orc, or Half Orc—they can't be Druids. They can do Shamans, but it's not exactly the same. I didn't want to do anything to lose my healing spells, but I don't like Priest or Paladins."

Horc nodded. "With you there."

"So, I opted for the Sand Elf. They're different from any Elf I've played before. They actually get a bonus for healing and a fire resistance. The drawback is most of my nature attack spells are sand-based."

"Sand-based?" Horc frowned and looked at Greensleeves. "What do you mean, 'sand-based?'"

"Exactly what it sounds like. I can summon a sand storm, a jet of sand, create a sand pit, do quicksand. I'm actually looking forward to trying some of these out."

"What about that tree-form you did?" Horc stopped walking and looked at his map. They'd walked past the dot for Thunderbow.

"Similar, but it now looks like dried drift wood, which I guess is better than a walking cactus." Greensleeves smiled.

"Yeah, there is that." Horc turned. "My trainer's supposed to be around here somewhere." He glanced at the signs and none of them made any sense to him.

"I guess another Druid Park is too much to ask since Orc don't have Druids." Greensleeves looked up and seemed to be studying the signs. He pursed his lips. "Does your dot look like it's in there?"

The sign above the door was a skeletal deer.

Horc compared their position with the map. "Yeah, I think so. What does that sign mean?"

"I bet they put the Skinning trainer with the Ranger trainer, 'cause all that deer makes me think of is either skinning or taxidermy, and I don't think we can be taxidermists in game."

"Probably not." Horc strolled toward the door.

The inside of the shop had a wide variety of animal hides hung on the wall. There were also a selection of skinning knives and bows alongside them. A gangly Orc sat on a stool, sharpening blades back in one corner with a huge pig at his side. Across from him, in the other back corner of the shop, was a meaner-looking Orc who was missing an eye and had a long scar that ended at a broken tusk on the right side of his face.

The yellow text above the gangly one read **Thunderbow, Orc Ranger, Level XXX**.

"Hello, Thunderbow?" Horc asked, drawing the two Orcs attention to him. "I'm Horc—Caleb Sureshot from Stone Helm City sent me to you. He said I need to learn about my Orc side."

Thunderbow set down the knife he'd been sharpening and seemed to study Horc. "Ranger Horc. Yes, I can see you need to learn what it is to be an Orc. Most halflings come to find the balance in their two sides before now. It may take a little while to get you to the point you need to be in your training so that the two sides of your soul are not conflicted."

Text flashed in front of Horc's vision.

Two Spirits in One Body

Complete

Rewards 5,000 XP

"Now that you've found me, I can instruct you on what it takes to be a Half Orc." Thunderbow waved his hand and a scroll appeared in it. "I have need of some supplies. If you would please get the items off this list for me, I would greatly appreciate it."

A quest box appeared.

Thunderbow's shopping
Rewards 4,000 XP
10 Silver
Accept-Decline

"Accept," Horc said. "Looks like we're going shopping."

He said his goodbyes to Thunderbow and headed out of the small shop, pausing at the Skinning trainer, an Orc name Quicknife.

"I have the Skinning profession," Horc said. "I forgot to check before leaving Stone Helm City. I think I may be in need of training."

Quicknife seemed to study him for a moment with his one remaining eye. "Yes, it might even be that you have some bad habits to unlearn. Do you have any skins on you that you've gotten from your kills, or have you sold them all already?"

Horc was about to say no, then he remembered the scorpion on the way to Red Wind Terrace. "Yeah, give me a second." He opened his bag and pulled out the carapace he'd gotten from the scorpion.

"No." Quicknife shook his head. "No one can really show their skill on bugs. Go out and bring me back five diamondback skins. They must be intact with no cuts save the one down the middle. Show me what you can do, Horc."

Display of skill
Collect five perfect diamondback skins for Quicknife
Rewards: Journeyman skinner
Accept-Decline

"Accept." Horc grinned at Quicknife. "Thank you. I'll be back shortly." He bowed slightly, then followed Greensleeves out of the shop.

"Let's take a look at Thunderbow's list," Greensleeves said, taking the scroll from Horc. After a moment he pursed his lips. "Yeah, this is going to take a little while. We'd better get started."

It was a different sort of quest from the ones he'd done in Stone Helm City, but Horc was in the mood for a change. "Is all of it here in the city?" He accepted the scroll back from Greensleeves.

"Looks that way. Let's go see what we can find. After we get this together, we'll see about finding you some snakes."

There were half a dozen items on the list. Horc glanced at his map. There were yellow dots all over the city. Greensleeves was right—they were going to be at it for a while, but he hoped by the end of it, he'd, at least, have a feeling for how the city was laid out and what was in the different sectors so he wouldn't have to rely on his map so heavily.

4

HORC PAUSED, as he and Greensleeves walked out of the Red Wind Terrace Apothecary, so he could check his map and see where the next closest dot was. Thunderbow's quest seemed to be taking them to every level of the terrace and along both sides of the canyon.

"Looks like we need to go up to the next level, but I can't figure out how we're supposed to get to one spot that looks like it's in the middle of the wall back there." Horc turned and pointed toward a spot on the far wall where there weren't any cliff-side businesses, just a wall of solid red rock.

"I'd bet there's some kind of passage or trail, or something that we haven't found a way into," Greensleeves said. "If we haven't sorted it out by the time we get everything on the list, maybe we can ask one of the guards wandering around."

"Okay." Horc walked toward the lift. They weren't as scary as they had been the first time he used one, but he still did his best to get as close as he could to the center of the platform each time he rode one. "Is it just me, or are there a lot more guards here in Red Wind Terrace than there were in Stone Helm?"

Greensleeves shrugged as they stopped to wait for the lift. From the way the chain was rattling, it was still coming up from ground level. "I think they stand out here more than they do there. Here they're bigger and meaner than most of the players. There, with so many human players running pallies, the guards in plate armor blend in more. But I bet the percentage of them is about the same."

The lift rattled to a stop on their level. Since it was going up, they got on.

"I guess that makes sense," Horc agreed. "But I still think the human guards are a bit bigger than players can get too."

"Probably. Makes them more imposing when Orc players start getting up high enough level to begin doing raids."

Horc frowned. "Raids? You mean like a group of opposing players attacking a city?"

The lift started up with a jerk. Horc resisted the urge to grab the central chain and hold on.

"Yeah, that's it," Greensleeves replied. "From what Rick says, they've got it set up already for parties to do raids, but players have to be a lot higher level before they can even think about it. I think he said minimum level for raiding is going to be seventy-five and we can't even get that high yet."

The lift stopped, and they got off.

"Yeah, we've got a ways to go before we reach that," Horc said. He glanced at his map and headed off in the direction of the dot. "Man, I always hate these quests where you have to go visit almost everyone on a space station before you get what you need."

Greensleeves chuckled. "Since Baladara isn't here, I'll say it for you… too much sci-fi."

"Thanks." Horc held back his laugh. His friends were always giving him grief about making too many references to sci-fi gaming when they were playing a fantasy game. Having the party who were rapidly becoming friends made it easier to forget the worry of the harrowing situation he was IRL.

Someone bumped into Horc as they were heading along the terrace to the next quest dot on the map. Horc stumbled toward the edge of the terrace and swayed hard. The blue sky above the canyon flashed in his sight as he spun, then he got a view of the ground floor of the city. He scrambled to keep his footing on the smooth sandstone of the terrace that didn't have any kind of wall or railing to keep people from falling off and a couple of stories down to the hard-packed walkways below. Something furry zipped by his face as a strong hand grabbed his wrist.

"I've got you," Greensleeves said. "Grab him."

With his heart pounding and trying to get his bearings, he wasn't sure exactly what Greensleeves was talking about. Horc flailed out in hopes of connecting with something, or someone. His fingers brushed against something soft, then hit leather. He closed his hand, hoping he was in time to avert disaster.

"Hey!" a man shouted. "Watch what you're grabbing."

Horc's arm lurched and felt like it was about to come out of its socket, but he held on.

Seconds later, Greensleeves had them back on the edge of the terrace. "Wow, that was close."

"Yeah." Horc's chest hurt from his heart pounding. "What happened?" He let go of the piece of leather armor he was holding onto and focused on the strange creature staring at him. It looked like some guy in a fur suit. Its face was tan fur with a dark brown marking that looked like a mask around its startling blue eyes. Sharp teeth set in a fierce, extended jaw were just inches from Horc's arm.

"We almost fell off the terrace," the beastman snarled. "I can't believe you're so clumsy you almost knocked us to our deaths." He shrugged. "Well, pseudo-deaths. It's a game. We all come back."

"Maybe, maybe not," Horc said. He looked at the letters above the beastman's head. **Tufkakes, Procyan,**

Rogue, Level 19. Horc frowned. "Okay, what's a Procyan?"

Tufkakes grinned, or at least Horc thought it was a grin. With a mouth that was more muzzle than mouth, and the rows of sharp teeth, it was hard to tell. "Can't you tell?" He stepped a little farther from the edge of the terrace and turned in a circle with his arms spread. He was dressed in dark gray leather armor, and had a ringed tail sticking out behind him.

They were in a fantasy game. Horc wasn't totally sure, although he had a good idea, but if Tufkakes had been what nearly knocked him to his death, he opted to try a less direct answer. "A rabbit?"

The grin on Tufkakes' muzzle turned into a frown. "No. I'm not some dumbass fluffy bunny."

"Panda?" Greensleeves joined in.

Tufkakes paused and a thoughtful line appeared on his forehead. "Okay, maybe, but no." He fumbled with something in his hands. It was a pale brown leather bag and it jingled slightly at the motion.

Horc patted his side and didn't feel his coin purse. He stared at Tufkakes and the coin purse in his hand. "Thief," Horc forced out in a hiss. "Raccoon. You're a thieving raccoon."

"What this?" Tufkakes held out the coin purse to Horc. "Nah, I didn't steal it. It flew around when we almost fell off the cliff and I stopped it from falling and spilling all the way down there." He gestured off the edge of the terrace and a couple of floors down toward the canyon floor.

"Thank you." Horc snatched the coin pouch back, and then stuck it in his backpack for extra security. He'd never stopped to think that players might try to steal from one another. It was something that didn't happen in his regular sci-fi game, Galactic Explorers. The fact that Tufkakes had nearly thrown him off the terrace in his attempt to get the coins in the purse irritated him even more. If he died because of some moron player, he was really going to be pissed off.

"Hey, no problem." Tufkakes put his hands behind his back and tilted his head in an obvious attempt to look innocent. "So, wait. Horc… was there a system announcement about you?"

"Yeah." Horc did his best to continue to look stern. "I'm the guy nobody's supposed to PVP with 'cause if I die, I might not survive IRL, or in game."

Tufkakes' demeanor instantly changed. "Oh, man. I'm really, really sorry. I didn't stop to check who I was near. I didn't mean for anything to happen. Honest. Look, you guys aren't running around with just the two of you, are you? If you're trying to stay alive, that might not be the best move. Will you let me make it up to you? I can be really helpful."

Horc stared at him, trying to understand what was going on. It was like the previous actions had all been a roleplay and they were looking at someone closer to the player's real-life persona.

"We've got a party," Greensleeves said. "Most of them can't come into Red Wind Terrace yet."

"Oh, I bet they're humans and have to get their rep with the Orcs up high enough to enter the city." From the level of excitement coming off him, Tufkakes was almost bouncing up and down. "Look. I can be a lot of help. Honest. I can. Do you have a Rogue yet? Particularly a Shadow Rogue?"

"No." Horc let out a long breath. He wasn't sure what a Rogue would be good for. If anything, he figured another Tank class would be better for protection. He wished Baladara was there. She was more familiar with fantasy games and would be able to make a better decision. He glanced at the party interface displaying on the right side of his vision. Her avatar and status bars were still grayed out.

"You're the right level to fit in with the rest of us," Greensleeves said. "Rogues can come in handy under the right circumstances."

Horc glanced at his friend. "So, you think it might be a good idea to expand the party? Even with someone who tried to steal from me?" He was always leery of trusting people who didn't start off on the right foot, or as in the cases of the other party members, people who'd needed help when they first met, and quickly proved themselves to be decent folks.

"Hey," Tufkakes objected, some of his earlier bravado coming back into his voice and stance as he squared his shoulders and glared. "I apologized for that. We should be past it."

"Maybe. But it might take me a while to warm up to you," Horc replied.

"Yeah, I think having another neutral party member and a rogue would be good." Greensleeves rubbed his chin. "He might've figured out those locks in the Gnoll King's Dungeon faster."

"You guys have done the Gnoll King's Dungeon? Wow." Tufkakes's eyes grew large. "The wiki says that dungeon is wicked bad. Even kicked out a party of execs from the California office."

"Not all of them. One of them is now part of our party," Greensleeves said.

"You're not all execs, are you?" Tufkakes but his hands in his pockets and shuffled his feet.

Horc laughed. "No. We're all sorts of people, IRL At least in here, we're all just players."

Greensleeves nodded. "And right now, we're all working toward keeping Horc alive while playing the game instead of him just sitting around in a tavern somewhere drinking until he's rescued."

"Right. Good for you." Tufkakes pulled his hands out of his pockets and held one out to Horc. "Look I really am sorry for almost pushing you off the ledge while picking your pocket. I'm a Rogue Procyan—it's sort of our thing. But if you guys take me on, I promise to not hit any of the party."

With more than a little trepidation, Horc returned Tufkakes' handshake. "Okay. I guess we could use another neutral player." Since Baladara was logged out, Horc was in charge of the party. He quickly sent Tufkakes an invite which the Rogue accepted.

Greensleeves patted Tufkakes on the shoulder. "Welcome to the party."

"Thanks." Tufkakes grinned, showing lots of sharp teeth. "Now let's hope we all survive the experience."

Inwardly, Horc groaned. Adding a rogue made sense, but he was still nervous about it. He had to remind himself it was just a game. As long as he survived long enough for the rescue team to get his pod out of the rubble of his house, he'd be fine.

5

HORC WALKED back into the small shop where Thunderbow was. He'd finished gathering everything on the Ranger trainer's shopping list and was ready to see what else the man with the pig companion had for him.

"Ah, so you've returned with my skins already?" Quicknife, the skinning trainer asked as Horc hurried past.

"What?" Horc stopped. "Ah, man. I totally forgot the skins. Give me a little while and I'll run out and get them for you." Tufkakes had shaken him up a bit and he'd totally forgotten about the five rattlesnake skins he was supposed to get.

"You cannot progress without them," Quicknife said and went pack to unrolling a huge hide to string onto a drying stand.

"Sorry we forgot about that," Greensleeves muttered softly from Horc's side. "New people can do that sometimes."

Horc gave him a quiet nod as he closed the distance to Thunderbow.

"You're a fast one, Horc," Thunderbow said as Horc began unloading the items he'd gathered. "That's good. There's a lot for the Rangers to do here in Red Wind Terrace. There is darkness growing in our world, and as of yet, we've not been able to determine its source. Some believe it originates in the neutral areas, places that are the most welcoming to your kind. After you have gathered the hides Quicknife has requested, I need you to journey to Tragiczan. My information tells me there may

be a source of darkness there, sitting on our borders.
Once there, seek out the darkness in whatever form it
takes and make sure it doesn't bother us any further."

Quest: Snuff out the Darkness
Travel to Tragiczan and find the trail to the source of
darkness there.
Rewards:
5,000 XP
Accept - Decline

"I'll do it," Horc said. He loved the fact that the
quest was going to take him back to where the rest of his
party was. He just hoped Baladara would've logged back
on, since she'd been with him from the beginning,
actually been the person who talked him into playing
Halfworld; he felt bad when he was playing and leveling
without her.

Thunderbow grinned. "You're a good man, Horc,
the Half Orc. Continue down this path and you will be
renowned amid the Rangers in no time."

"That'd be nice." Horc glanced at Greensleeves and
Tufkakes. "You two need anything else in town before
we head out?"

Tufkakes glanced around the shop like he was
casing the joint, but he shook his head. "I think I'm
good."

"I've got my supplies," Greensleeves said.

"Okay." Horc walked out of the small shop and
headed for the open-air lift for the ride down to ground
level and they moved out to collect some snake skins. In
the time they'd been in Red Wind Terrace, it seemed like
there were more and more players, just like when they'd
been in Stone Helm City. "I would've figured folks
would be going to work at some point," Horc said as they
cleared the gate of the city, nearly getting run down by a
huge Orc Warrior.

"Depends on what office they're out of," Tufkakes said. "Most of us in the US have already spent our Monday grinding at the cube farm."

Horc stopped and stared at him. "Wait. It's Monday evening already? But I haven't been in here that long, have I?"

Greensleeves nodded. "All weekend and then some. We're just trying not to remind you about it."

"But shouldn't they have gotten to my pod by now? This doesn't make sense." Horc's head spun. He knew it had taken more than a day for the rescue team to reach his house, since he'd made it clear they were to be helping other people first. He was safe in the game…well, at least not bleeding out under the weight of his collapsed house. But he figured they would've reached him already. How long did it take to move the rubble of a house to reach someone trapped in their gaming pod?

"I totally forgot to give you an update." Greensleeves patted Horc's arm. "Rick told me the retrieval team was moving fairly slow in getting to your pod. The damage to your house is extensive and they don't want to inadvertently cause a spark. There's a lot of open gas lines in the area."

"Open gas lines? You mean like when that tornado took Kansas City down to the bedrock?" Hearing about the level of destruction made everything a lot worse. In Kansas City it had taken months before the area was totally safe due to ruptured gas lines, broken pipelines, and live electrical wires making things dangerous for rescuers and demo teams to go in and start repairing the carnage.

Greensleeves pursed his lips and nodded. "That's right. But it's not exactly that bad. This wasn't that powerful of a storm. There are at least some buildings in

Mesquite and Garland still partially standing. There was nothing left of Kansas City."

"Right." Horc let out a long sigh. "Right. They're working on it. I'm going to be fine. I have to keep telling myself that, or I'll go bonkers."

"And that won't help anyone," Tufkakes said. "We just soldier on."

"Good idea," Greensleeves said. "We've got some snakes to find, kill and skin so you can get your training."

Horc pushed down the panic attack that threatened to overwhelm him. He'd been doing great for a couple of days, so finding out his rescue was taking longer than he'd expected it to shouldn't cause him to totally freak out. He needed to focus on just playing the game until it was time for him to rejoin the real world.

STARING AT his map, Horc frowned. They were in the middle of the shaded area that indicated it was where the object of their quest should be, but they hadn't found any diamondbacks to kill and skin. They'd battled a number of scorpions of various flavors, a few feral pigs and a pack of Sun Wolves, but hadn't found their objectives.

"We're in the right place." He swiped and dismissed the map. "I wonder if we need to start rolling over rocks and looking there."

"Or maybe check in the shadows." Tufkakes headed toward the wall of the canyon they were in. "If these snakes are like real life snakes, then they might be seeking out shade in the heat of the day."

"Rick keeps saying the programmers went out of their way to make things as life-like as possible." Greensleeves followed their new party member. "So, the game snakes acting more like snakes IRL, makes sense."

As he and his wolf headed after them, Horc didn't bother pointing out that animals IRL tended to run from people as opposed to attacking them like the game critters did. But if the game animals ran from them, he'd feel like crap chasing them down to kill them, particularly things like the feral pigs and the wolves.

"Ah, here you go." Tufkakes pointed to something a short distance away, then flung a knife at it.

On Horc's screen, his avatar flashed with a red glow indicating he was in combat. Seconds later a huge rattlesnake slithered out of the shadows. **Desert Diamondback, Level 25** shone in red letters above it. It was a couple of levels above them, but Horc was fairly sure with three players and the wolf attacking it, there wasn't going to be much of a challenge.

"Shit!" Tufkakes recoiled from the snake's attack. "It's got poison… of course, it's got poison." He flung another knife as Horc got off an Impact arrow.

Horc's wolf hit the snake hard.

"I've got you." Greensleeves cast a quick spell with a purple glow.

Horc got off another arrow. It took Horc three more arrows, while his wolf was chewing on it and Tufkakes was hacking at it.

When it finally stopped moving, Tufkakes glared down at it as he stepped back. "Okay. That was irritatingly hard. It's a damned snake. It shouldn't have taken so much to put down."

"But it was a strong snake." Greensleeves pulled out a flask and took a swig. Instantly his mana bar in the group icons flashed back to full.

"At least all I need is five skins," Horc said, getting up next to the small monster. "It's not like the quests to collect twenty-five of something."

Tufkakes's eyes grew large. "Twenty-five? Damn. Not cool. I think the most I've had to collect for one quest is ten, and with the drop rate those rats had on fangs, it took me a couple of hours to complete."

Greensleeves wrinkled his nose. "Rat fangs? Really? But then we've had body parts, but they're normally bigger than rat fangs."

Tufkakes retrieved his daggers and wiped them down before slipping them in his sheaths. "They were fairly large rats."

"Must've been." Horc looted the snake. A set of fangs, dripping in venom. A curled tail, and a couple of silvers. Then he set about skinning it. He got a pile of mangled scraps from it. Nothing flashed for it being part of his quest. "Well, looks like this is going to be a bit of a challenge."

"Keeps the game interesting," Tufkakes said. "Let's see about finding the next one."

TWENTY SNAKES later, Horc had the skins he needed. "Okay. I'm starting to think some of this is just for wasting time." He wiped his skinning knife off before returning it to the sheath on his belt.

Tufkakes shrugged. "It's a game. It's supposed to be for wasting time. At least these guys got me to level 20."

"He's got a point." Greensleeves chuckled.

"Yah, I can see that." Halfworld was so lifelike, Horc had trouble remembering that he liked wasting time in games. Sure, he was accomplishing things like growing in levels, and getting more in-game gold, but with the reality feel of it, he kept thinking he needed to be making more strides toward something.

"Alright, let's go turn this in so we can go meet up with the others in Tragiczan," Greensleeves said, turning toward the mouth of the canyon.

AS HE completed Quicknife's quest, Horc's screen flashed with:

Journeyman Skinner achieved

"You have the potential to be a great leather worker, Horc." Quicknife rolled up the snake skins and slipped them into a pack on the ground near his chair. "Come back to me when you're ready for more training."

"Of course." Horc nodded slightly. He had no idea when he was going to need training in skinning again and wasn't sure where he'd be when that happened. He wouldn't waste the time traveling all the way to Red Wind Terrace if there was a spot closer that he could get his training at.

Hey, where are you guys? Baladara appeared in their group chat.

Red Wind Terrace. Greensleeves. *Slasher and Steelmaiden are in Tragiczan waiting for us. The next round of quests takes us back there.*

I'm already in Tragiczan, but they aren't here. Baladara.

Are they nearby? Horc added as he and Greensleeves walked out of the shop Quicknife and Thunderbow shared. *They said they were going to try to find some quests in that area that would help their rep with the Orcs.*

Look at your party icons. They show on. When I check their location, it shows in Tragiczan. When I got here I went to the Inn, since that looks to be where they are, but they aren't here. Baladara.

I wonder if there's some kind of system glitch or phasing at work. Greensleeves.

Phasing. Oh, that would be a royal pain. I hate phasing. Baladara

Me too. Tufkakes.

Yeah, I wanted to talk to you about adding more party members when I'm not around. Baladara.

Hey Tufkakes. Baladara.

Hi Baladara. Heard nice things about you. Tufkakes.

Stay there. We're on our way back now. Horc glanced at Greensleeves as they approached the lift. "Any idea where the Rogue trainer Tufkakes went to see is?"

"Hang on." Greensleeves got a faraway look as they stopped for the platform to arrive.

Guys, I'll meet you at the gate. Tufkakes.

Thanks. Horc replied. "Don't worry, he's on the way."

"Right." The lift arrived and they both stepped on. "Do me a favor and keep an eye on me while I check with Rick on strange server things like phasing. He hadn't said anything about parties getting out of synch due to various quests and things like you find in other games."

"Sure." Horc hoped Greensleeves wasn't going to fully log out and talk with Rick—just use text or something. If he logged out, they might be stuck riding the lift up and down for a little while and the open-air contraption still made Horc a little bit fearful of falling to his death from the wooden platform that was bereft of any kind of security device to keep the passengers from falling off it.

As the lift went down, Greensleeves got that glassy-eyed look again. It lasted for the whole trip down to the ground level, then he blinked as the platform shook, indicating they'd arrived.

"Okay. Rick's looking into it. He says there shouldn't be any phasing at this point in the plot. It's too big of a hassle and too many people don't like it, even if it does advance the story line." They hurried off the round wooden conveyance before it started up again. "But he said it does sound like something's wrong on the servers if they're showing in the inn and aren't there."

"Not good," Horc said as they headed toward the gate, weaving their way through the ever-growing flood of people in the game. He wondered if word had gotten out over the weekend and even employees of Total Immersion Systems who didn't normally play games had opted to give it a shot to get the bonus for helping spot bugs in the beta. If part of their party had disappeared from the Inn he'd left them at, that was a pretty big bug.

Up ahead, Tufkakes stood on a large rock near the gate, his paw-like hand over his dark eyes as if he was scanning the crowd for them.

"You know he could just use the map and watch the character dots to determine where people were at before resorting to scanning the ground like this," Greensleeves said.

"Maybe he's just having fun," Horc replied.

"Probably," Greensleeves agreed. "Makes sense to me. Or maybe he's still twelve."

"And signed on with his father's credentials. That could be." Horc waved back and Tufkakes jumped off the rock. One of the things about video games was there was no way to tell anything about the players IRL.

"Okay, let's keep moving," Tufkakes said as they headed out the gate. "Didn't you say something while we were hunting those damned snakes about it being about an hour's hike from Red Wind Terrace to Tragiczan?"

"That's right. If we're lucky and don't run into any problems along the way." Horc said as his wolf took the lead, seeming to know the way.

"Problems might slow us down, but they should at least be worth some XP," Tufkakes said with a grin.

"There is that," Greensleeves agreed.

Horc was growing worried about Slasher and Steelmaiden. He hoped Rick would be able to find out something about what had happened to them. Maybe they'd just logged out and the system was stuck on them still being in Tragiczan. He wanted to get there quickly and find out. As he walked, he remembered he had a quest to root out the evil forces that were in the small settlement. Could those forces somehow be responsible for his friends' problems?

6

BY THE time they reached Tragiczan, Horc was more than ready for a shower. The desert sand seemed to stick to him worse than it had before. He wasn't sure, but it felt like it was caking up around his pack and in every crevice in his gear it could find.

The little settlement looked much as it had when he'd been there before, except the sun was approaching the horizon, so most of the vendors had closed their shops. He was a little surprised by that since he hadn't noticed that in either Stone Helm City, or in Red Wind Terrace. The larger cities seemed to be like most game cities and open all the time.

"Okay, so at least I can see you guys." Baladara leaned against the entrance of the inn. The little elf looked more like Mike, the guy behind the toon, than she normally did. Something about the pose and the grumpy look on her delicate features screamed male human.

"And we can see you," Greensleeves countered.

"Okay, what did you do to yourself?" Baladara asked looking Greensleeves over from head to toe.

"Rick pulled some strings and let me change my race. I prefer Elves over Humans anyway, and this way I'm neutral like Horc." Greensleeves turned around in a tight circle. "Do you like the new look?"

"Very desert." Baladara nodded. "But yeah, a better look than the basic human. Why didn't you do that to start with?"

"Rick wanted me to go human and go through the Gnoll King's Dungeon." Greensleeves shrugged. "You know, sometimes we do what we can to keep the spouses happy."

"I hear you. Lisa was happy with the downtime I took." Baladara looked at Tufkakes. "And you managed to pick up your own personal stuffed animal while I was out."

Tufkakes bared his teeth. "I'm a Procyan, not a stuffed animal."

"Okay. Well, we did need a Rogue. I guess you'll do."

"Thanks. I didn't know all the new party members needed approval first." Tufkakes put his hands on his hips. "I realized who Horc is and wanted to help."

"Also, he almost knocked me off one of the terraces trying to pick my pocket," Horc muttered.

Baladara looked Tufkakes up and down, more sternly than she had Greensleeves' new toon. "Okay then. I'll keep my eye on you."

"He's a good Rogue," Greensleeves said. "And like you said, we need one in the party. Oh, wait a second." He got the distant look indicating he was getting something on his screen. After a couple of seconds, he blinked. "That's not good. Okay. Rick said he and the development team have checked. Slasher and Steelmaiden are still logged in. Although their signals are coming from the inn, as far as in-game players can tell, they're really trekking across the desert to the west of here. Right now, they're several hours out."

Baladara rolled her eyes. "So, it's a server glitch?"

"Or something." Greensleeves blinked a couple of times. "Rick says they are currently querying the game AI to see if it knows what's going on. That might take a while. He's set up a bypass so we can find them on our maps."

A green arrow appeared on the edge of the map in the upper right of Horc's vision. When they got close enough, it would change to a dot. Horc waved to make the map grow larger. He had to do it several times before he could get the arrow to go away. "Looks like they're heading to the western shore. What level is that area?"

Greensleeves frowned. "Looks like twenty-five to thirty. Might be a bit of a challenge."

Horc pursed his lips. "And I didn't take time to find an enchanter in Red Wind Terrace to find out about doing something to re-empower my axe."

Baladara shook her head. "You're such a newb. Okay, if we're heading out after them, it might be a good idea to be totally stocked up on potions, drinks, and food, as well as getting that axe to do something beyond just looking cheap. We can get the food and drink here, but I think everyone else has folded up for the night. Do we want to wait, or do you guys want to go back to Red Wind, then meet me on the road?"

Greensleeves frowned. "I don't like the idea of splitting the party again. That's not working out so great. Let's get what we can here and head out, unless Horc and Tufkakes want to grab a bed for a few hours and then take off."

"The desert will be cooler at night," Tufkakes said. "Let's see how far we can get."

Although Horc couldn't find a problem in the logic, his feet hurt, and he wanted to get the sand out of and off of everything. "Sounds like a plan," he muttered, hoping he wasn't going to live to regret it, but they needed to find out what was up with Steelmaiden and Slasher.

They headed into the inn to resupply what they could. The party cleared the door, when one of the barmaids slammed it shut.

"Thank you for finally getting inside," she said as she forced locks shut.

"What's going on?" Horc asked, not liking the idea of being locked in. It was going to slow them down getting on the trail to find the rest of their party.

"Oh,"—the barmaid looked around and stammered—"we're just ready to close up for the night." She paused and studied Horc. "Hey. I remember you—you have a room here with those other two. The Warrior and the Barbarian woman."

"That's right. You wouldn't happen to know what happened to them, after I left?" Horc suddenly hoped that maybe someone had seen or heard something that would give them some answers as to what was going on.

The barmaid shook her head a little more enthusiastically than she needed to, then waved them down the steps into the main room. "No, they went out yesterday and never came back."

That played with what they were seeing on the map but it didn't make sense. Horc thought about taking a little while and trying to see if anyone else would tell them more, but he wanted to get their supplies and get on the road, if the barmaid would let them out of the door.

"Do you know if they talked to anyone before they left Tragiczan?" Greensleeves asked.

She shook her head again. "I didn't see them after they left the inn."

Tufkakes walked around the barmaid. "They need to work on these NPCs. It's like the AI is still trying to figure out what they should be saying. If we're far enough into the development that we're beta testing, it shouldn't be this clunky."

"Then luckily, we've got a short cut to the designers." Greensleeves grinned. "But go ahead and fill out a bug report. It has more impact coming from multiple people."

"We want to get some supplies and leave," Horc said, trying to focus on the barmaid while his friends talked. "We need to find the rest of our party."

"They haven't been seen-" she started again.

"Since they left the inn," Baladara finished for her. "Yeah, you already said that. We get it. We just want provisions and we'll be out of your hair."

"It's really dangerous to be outside at night." The barmaid put her hands in her blue apron and looked at the floor. "People are disappearing."

A message flashed on Horc's screen.

Quest Completed: Snuff out the Darkness
Travel to Tragiczan and find the trail to the source of darkness there.
Rewards:
5,000 XP

Horc's XP bar flashed and grew longer. Then another message popped up

Quest: Snuff out the Darkness
Follow the trail of darkness and find out where it leads.
Rewards:
5,000 XP
Accept - Decline

"Accept," Horc muttered under his breath.

"Accept what?" Baladara asked.

"Apparently, talking with the barmaid here was the completion of the first part of the quest chain to find the source of darkness in Tragiczan. We're supposed to follow the trail and find out where it leads." Horc didn't like things that weren't fairly direct and laid out for him, particularly when he was in a game and supposed to be relaxing.

"And you didn't think to share that quest with those of us who didn't get it?" Baladara asked with her hands on her hips.

Sharing quests wasn't something he was used to in the other games he played. "How do I do that?"

"Pull up the quest details," Baladara instructed. "There should be a share option."

Doing what she said, he spotted the button. When he tapped share, a message popped up.

The quest isn't available for sharing.

"Not an option," Horc relayed.

Baladara pouted slightly.

"I wonder if Steelmaiden and Slasher were taken as part of this quest," Greensleeves muttered as he headed for the main room and the bar.

"That sounds a little strange," Horc replied, following him. "Wouldn't that mean the AI kidnapped them or something?"

"Although I don't want you hurt, I cannot keep you here." The barmaid rushed past them. "It might be a long quest, so let me stock you up."

"Thanks." Tufkakes leaned against the bar when they got across the main room.

"I don't know much about the AI. While you guys restock, I'll check with Rick and see if this might be something that's been programmed." Greensleeves pulled out a few coins. "This should cover my part."

"I wish we all had spouses who were programmers," Baladara said. "Would make it a lot easier for things in the game."

"I don't think he's trying to cheat," Horc said, then told the barmaid what they were going to need.

"Then what do you call the new race?" Baladara pulled out a few coins to help pay for her part.

"Trying to help me stay alive." Horc hadn't really thought about that being a form of cheating. There were several games he'd heard about that for a little extra cash, players could change things about their toons without losing their levels and belongings.

"It's nice having friends who are willing to pull strings for you," Tufkakes added his part of the coins as the barmaid began putting their order on the counter and they divided up the food, drink, and a couple of potions.

"Which reminds me," Baladara turned from the barmaid and focused on Tufkakes. "We all know who each of us is IRL, but who are you? All we know is your handle of Tufkakes. What kind of name is Tufkakes?"

"I kinda combined the name of a character in a song to come up with it. I really liked the song and when I saw that Procyans are basically humanoid raccoons, it made sense." Tufkakes looked more uncomfortable than he had since Horc had met him.

"Ooookaaaaay, so who are you IRL?" Baladara pushed. "My name's Mike Simmons from the Dallas office."

Tufkakes nodded. "You're a guy in real life, huh…I guess that explains some of the attitude."

Baladara frowned. "Attitude? I don't have an attitude, and this isn't about me—it's about you."

"Fine. My name's Shelia Green. I'm out of the Houston office."

"Shelia, didn't we meet at one of the big company training sessions a couple of years ago? You're in the billing department. In case you forgot from the server message, I'm Alan Gosling." Horc put the last of his part of the supplies into his bag.

"Alan Gosling, yes we did, now that you mention it." Tufkakes put his part of the supplies away.

"Okay, Shelia, I like looking at girls when I play, rather than boys, what's your excuse?" Baladara continued to grill her.

"I get tired of the general pompous attitude of a lot of the guys who play these games. For years, when I play a female character, I get hit on a lot by guys who probably look and act a lot worse than their avatars IRL.

After I got tired of being invited to harems every few days, I started playing male toons. One of the things I like about Halfworld is there are enough non-human races I can find things that are male, but still give me a little female feel." He ran his hand through the brown fur on his arm. "Some of these games have toons that aren't really male or female in any real sense."

"Well said," Greensleeves said, drawing attention to himself.

"Tufkakes, you're safe with us, no matter what sex you want to be," Horc said. He always hated it when gamers substituted their in-game lives for their real ones and thought they were all kinds of hot stuff when they really weren't.

Tufkakes grinned. "Thanks. It really amazes me that you're holding yourself together so well when your real life is hanging by a thread."

"Can't do much else." Horc turned to Greensleeves. "What did you find out?"

"Rick doesn't have much. The game AI isn't supposed to be going around kidnapping players, but that doesn't mean there aren't bugs in the system."

"Right," Baladara said. "So, I guess we catch up to Steelmaiden and Slasher and see what's going on."

"Rick's working on something that'll help with that." Greensleeves glanced at the remaining pile of supplies on the bar. "I guess these are mine?"

Horc nodded. "Figured you could carry your own stuff. What's Rick working on?"

"Well, I asked if we could either get a special case, so we could get mounts, or if we could get a level boost so we can ride."

"Yeah, level boosts would be awesome." Tufkakes fist pumped and grinned.

Greensleeves shook his head. "Sorry, can't pull that off without approval from higher up. But he is going to arrange for us some transport but we won't be riding mounts."

"Not riding mounts?" Baladara frowned. "And what does that mean exactly?"

"He wouldn't say—just that I'd probably like it a lot." Greensleeves finished putting his supplies away. "Let's head out into the center of town and see what he's worked up."

Again, the barmaid ran ahead of us. "I really don't think this is a good idea." She touched the door and started to raise the beam locking us in.

"We're players, sweetie," Tufkakes said. "We'll be fine."

The beam cleared the thick iron brackets holding it against the doors and something hit them hard from outside. The room shook. Horc's wolf growled, and Horc reflexively grabbed his axe. It might look cheap, but it still had a good edge and could do some damage.

7

THE DOOR shuddered again, then when the next blow hit, it flew open. The cold desert night air flooded in around them as they the party griped their weapons and prepared their spells.

There was nothing there.

"Okay. What's happening here?" Horc peered into the darkness, wishing the torches in the inn hadn't been so bright and that night hadn't fallen so fast and bleak outside the building.

"Not sure." Baladara's hands glowed a soft yellow. "But let's shed some light on the situation."

"I don't see anything out here," Tufkakes' voice came from outside the door.

"How did he get out there?" Baladara asked as she finished the spell she'd started, and light erupted just beyond the door.

"Damn! Warn me next time." Tufkakes sounded pained.

"Same to ya," Baladara retorted.

"It's Shadowwalking and, when you do something like that, I can't do it. Okay." Tufkakes appeared at the edge of the door, then his eyes widened. "Shit. It's right here." He threw two knives quickly.

"Right where?" Baladara ran through the door with Horc, his wolf, and Greensleeves right on her heels.

A huge skeletal shadow standing nearly ten feet tall towered just to the side of the door. Above the monster were the words **Sand Giant Shadow Level 30** with a single star next to the name.

"Freaking great." Baladara got off a fireball. "The shadow of a giant. Not what we need right now."

"And it's a special critter too." Greensleeves' Druid spell was a dusty brown as it flew toward the giant.

Horc stopped just outside the door as his wolf rushed the monster. He fired an Flaming Impact arrow.

The shadow howled in pain as the flaming arrow coated in spells struck. Its health dropped a bit, but not much. Horc had no idea whose attack did the most damage.

As the next round of spells went off, Tufkakes, who Horc hadn't even realized had vanished again, appeared behind the shadow and managed to run up its leg before plunging a knife into its ribs from behind. More points came off its health.

For the next few minutes, Horc didn't bother keeping track of who was doing what damage to the thing; he just loosed arrow after arrow at it. When his mana was high enough, he hit it with spell arrows, but they drained him quickly. Baladara and Greensleeves pounded on it with their magics while Tufkakes and Horc's wolf worked at it up close and personal.

When its health had dropped to flashing orange, it flung Tufkakes and the wolf aside and took off toward the far side of the village.

"Oh no, you don't." Horc held his arrow and focused his shot on the shadow's head. His mana flashed indicating he could add Flame to his Impact arrow. He let it fly. The bonus buff for the careful aim added damage to the blow. Along with the Impact arrow slowing it, the flames burning it caused the giant shadow to stumble. Horc's wolf dashed back in and grabbed at its leg.

With a loud bellow, the giant crashed to the ground.

"Gotcha!" Tufkakes threw himself on the dark form that struggled to rise again. His knives did a lot of damage as he struck blow after blow on the thing.

Two more spells from Baladara and Greensleeves had its health flashing and Horc finished it off with a Razor arrow that managed to cut through the thing's neck before embedding itself into the wall of the house across from it.

Tufkakes stood up and shook himself, looking for a moment like Horc's wolf who was doing the same thing. Dirt and dust flew around them.

"I've got you, Tufkakes." Greensleeves' spell glow turned from brown to blue as he healed Tufkakes, who, with the wolf had taken the most damage in the fight. He'd nearly died; he was so slow.

"Thanks," Tufkakes said as he started looting the shadow.

Horc cast his Heal Pet spell to bring his wolf up to max, then tossed him a chunk of meat for good measure. "That was intense." Horc slung his bow over his shoulder as his coin purse rang and felt heavier.

"At least it only had one star," Baladara said, pulling out a drink and sitting down. "Almost made me feel like we were back in the dungeon, and that was no fun."

"But we got cool stuff," Horc said, opening his own flask to bring his mana back up to max.

"Dungeons suck," Tufkakes said. "Tried one near the starting zone and that was a complete PITA."

Horc frowned. "Pita?"

"Pain in the ass." Tufkakes grinned. "Sorry. I know I have a bit of a mouth on me, and I'm always fussing at the kids about cussing."

"And it doesn't help, does it?" Baladara replied. "I get you there."

A bright glow erupted from the center of the town square and a carriage complete with a driver and four-in-hand team of horses stood there. The horses were huge beasts that glistened shiny black in the remnants of Baladara's light spell. The carriage was an open affair that looked like it was ready for a loving couple to take a blanket covered ride around a winter park. It wasn't anything Horc expected to find in a game.

"Okay, now, that's cool." Baladara stood and started toward it. "Is this what Rick was working on for us?"

"It is," the driver grinned down at them. There wasn't any text over his head and something in his bearing reminded Horc of Miranda, the developer who'd been keeping tabs on him and had actually been the one to defeat the Gnoll King in the final battle of the dungeon. The developers were a little out of sync with the rest of the game world and it set them apart, almost like gods. This one was even overly handsome with wavy blond hair, high cheekbones, broad shoulders and perfect teeth.

"Hey Rick!" Greensleeves ran over to the carriage. "How did you pull this off?"

"It's my own personal vehicle. There's a few places in game where even the developers can't just pop in. So, we all have our own steeds and such." Rick gestured to the horses. "You know I'm not much of an animal person, and I could've designed my own motorcycle or car, or something, but this reminded me of that carriage from our wedding."

Greensleeves grinned foolishly. "Oh my god. It does. You're too much."

"Well, you guys get in." Rick gestured to the back of the open-air carriage. "I can't stay in game too long. We're still looking into the AI acting up."

Horc gave Baladara a hand up into the powder-blue cushioned seat, then settled in beside her. His wolf sat at his feet, and Tufkakes sat opposite them as Greensleeves hopped up on the driver's bench next to Rick.

"Alright, everyone, hold on. I don't promise this will be smooth." Rick picked up the reins, snapped them, and yelled "Yee-haa!"

The horses reared and took off at a high speed. Dust flew up around them. Horc glanced back toward the inn. The door was already closed, and he had no doubt it was probably barred on the inside too. There were no signs of anyone in the little village. Even during their battle, no one had stepped out to see what was going on. It all fell quickly behind them as Rick's carriage carried them away and out into the desert night.

"We may have figured out why Slasher and Steelmaiden can't log out," Rick said as they rode along.

"Why?" Greensleeves responded.

"They're stuck in combat." Rick flicked his wrists, shaking the reins to urge the horses to greater speed.

"Why should that matter?" Horc asked. He'd never tried to log out during a fight—it always sounded like a way to cheat.

"Game rules," Baladara said. "Actually, that's the rules in most games. If you're in combat, you have to finish the combat before you can log out. Keeps people honest. Think about that moron Stan from the mailroom. I bet if he was losing a fight, he'd log out to get away from it, then log back in when he thought it was safe."

"Exactly," Rick added. "We're not totally sure how they're locked in combat."

Horc glanced at their icons in the party list. "Neither one of them is losing health points, but they both seem down."

"Exactly. It's almost like they are stuck in a state of being harmed just enough that their normal regeneration is covering the damage, so they aren't falling too far." Rick looked a little uncomfortable as the carriage bounced along.

"But if they weren't in pods and stuck in combat, wouldn't they eventually die from the stress of the VR gear keeping them on their feet for a long time?" Baladara asked, looking at her own hands as if wondering what would happen to her if she was the one they'd misplaced.

"We don't have studies on that," Rick said. "We might have to keep an eye on things if it looks like any of you are stuck in the game. We're already monitoring Alan for everything that happens. Hopefully we'll have more good news soon."

"I hope so," Greensleeves said as Horc settled himself into the seat and crossed his arms to attempt to relax on their journey.

Horc's screen flashed, indicating he had a new text. Since all he was doing was riding in the carriage, he decided to look at it.

Alan, how are you doing? We haven't heard from you in a couple of days. Mom

I'm fine. Still stuck in the game. They're supposed to be working on getting my pod out of the house.

Your father and I have tried to get in there and lend a hand, but we can't get past the barricades they have set up on 75. Mom

Don't worry about it. Have you guys found a hotel yet?

Yes. We're settling in there nicely. It's a bit pricy, but it was all we could find. Mom

He hated the idea of his folks spending too much money just to be close when he came out of the pod. *If it would be better for you guys to head home, I'll understand. I could come visit when I get out of here.*

No. We're staying right where we're at. It's not like we don't have plenty of cash stashed away in case of emergencies. Mom

We don't know how long this is going to take. I don't want you stressing yourself out. He'd feel terrible if something happened to either of his folks due to stress of him being in his predicament.

We'll be fine. Your father has found some guys who like to sit around watching old war movies, so he's happy among his people. He's promised to take me shopping at the Galleria tomorrow, so that will be nice. We're finding things to do—just wish you were here with us. Mom

Me too. As they let me know how they're coming on digging me out, I'll pass it along.

Thanks. We'll be there when you wake up, if they let us. Mom

They better. He hadn't even thought of that. What would he do if they didn't want him having visitors when he woke up? It wasn't like he'd been in a horrible accident and was going to emerge disfigured or anything. He was just stuck in his pod and it was protecting him from the wreckage of his house. But he was in the pod a lot longer than most people ever were. He wasn't sure how long it would take before his muscles started to atrophy and things like that. He hoped it would be more than a week.

Oh, your father just came back. We need to go to dinner. You take care and don't die in that game. I'll talk to you later. Mom.

I'll do my best. You guys have a good meal.

We will. It'll be better when you're here to eat with us. Mom

Your father says hi. Mom

Tell Dad hi for me too

Talk to you later. Mom.

You bet. Horc hoped he wasn't lying to his mother. The longer it took them to reach his pod, the more worried he became. There were too many unknowns, too many chances for something to go wrong. The text window faded and Horc kept his eyes closed, letting the easy movements of the carriage lull him to sleep. With any luck, he'd wake up, get the notification they'd exhumed his pod, and he was going to be able to rejoin the world of the living.

8

THE SLOWING of the carriage brought Horc out of his slumber. It had been over a day, in-game, since he'd had any rest, and he was more tired than he expected. But everyone else had been able to get out of the game for a while and actually rest their bodies in real life. He didn't have that luxury.

"Looks like this is the end of the road for the moment," Rick said. "I knew I probably couldn't take you guys all the way, but I was at least able to knock a good chunk off your travels. I've got to go see what they've dug up on the AI." He glanced at Greensleeves. "I'll let you know what we found out. Since we can't take the game down until Alan is out of his pod, if we have to tweak the AI, that's going to take everyone working together."

Greensleeves nodded. "I understand. Thanks for the lift."

Rick pulled the team to a stop. "You guys try not to take on anything too far over your levels but have fun till we get everything worked out."

"Okay." Greensleeves gave him a long look before jumping off the seat and landing in the sand the carriage's wheels were sitting in. "Take care of yourself. I'm in a pod and it'll keep me going. You're not. You need sleep."

"Yes, mother." Rick flashed him a bright smile and then he and the carriage faded away.

After a moment of silence, Baladara started walking across the dunes. "I guess we keep going the direction we have been. One thing we need to tell these developers is more landmarks in the landscape, even in the deserts."

Tufkakes laughed. "I'm not sure Rick is going to want to give us rides again. We spent most of the time telling him what's wrong with his game."

"Nah," Greensleeves said. "He likes hearing what people think of his work. He doesn't get to talk to players other than me very often. Plus, you guys told him a lot about what you liked too."

Horc yawned and rolled his shoulders. The game was real enough—he even felt like he had a slight crick in his neck from falling asleep in the carriage. "Sounds like I missed a bit."

Baladara shook her head. "Not really. We were just filling Rick in on what we thought the game should be like. I've never talked to a game designer before; that was interesting."

"Wait a minute, guys." Tufkakes paused and looked around. "Is it just me, or is something shaking the ground?"

Horc tried to feel what Tufkakes was talking about. There was a slight quivering sensation coming up through his feet and legs. "Yeah. Almost like there's a train coming."

"Or a big rig," Greensleeves said.

Baladara's eyes got big and she pointed over Horc's shoulder. "Or a really big worm." She started casting a spell, and her hands glowed red.

Horc unslung his bow and reached for an arrow as he turned to see what she was pointing at. A huge worm rose out of the sand dune and towered over them.

"All right, I'm not sure I like running with you guys," Tufkakes complained as he pulled out daggers and began throwing them. "It's giant shadow beasts and giant worms. Neither of which are fun."

Casting Flame on his Razor arrow, Horc got off his first attack and his wolf raced across the sand to hit the worm at the same time as the others' attacks. "Can't say I'd blame you. Things just seem to be getting harder."

"It's that we're in the middle of the desert and not on a road," Baladara snapped as she started her next spell. "If we were on the road, we'd be fine, or at least run into fewer things. But someone's husband had to drop us off in the middle of the wilderness and now we get to fight our way back to safety."

Greensleeves got his first spell off. "I'll advise him of your displeasure at dropping us where he did. He might add a few monsters along the road to make things harder, if that's how you like it."

"I don't like things harder," Baladara shouted as her spell left her fingers. "I think that's your thing."

As Horc got off his second arrows, he looked at the worm and the red text above its head. **Dunediver, Level 32**. At least it didn't have any stars next to its name. But their attacks didn't seem to be having a ton of effect on it. After two rounds of solid hits, its health was barely affected.

"Try concentrating our shots on its head," Horc suggested as he pulled an Impact arrow and added Poison to it. Even if the damage-over-time spells weren't instant hurt on the thing, it would add up and weaken it as stronger spells hit it.

He managed to hit it in the center of the head. The worm straightened to its full height, a good ten to twelve feet, and an eerie scream came out of it. The hit dropped its health bar farther, but it still wasn't even down a quarter of its points. If any of them had stumbled across it by themselves, it would've killed them quickly and then gone back to diving through the dunes.

"Easier said than done, Ranger." Tufkakes took off running, looking like he was trying to flank the beast, so he could attack it from behind.

Baladara and Greensleeves' next attacks were good head shots, doing more damage than the previous strikes had. The worm finally dropped to nearly a half and it dove into the sand.

"Oh no you don't." Tufkakes jumped on it as it went past him. He drove his knives into the base of the worm's skull. The hits were good and knocked it down to just below half health.

Horc's Poison arrow spell finished its cooldown, and he added it to the next Razor arrow he fired. With the worm thrashing, trying to get back into the dune, but acting like there was something wrong with it, he had trouble getting a good shot to the head. He slowed down. Focusing his shots, he managed to get another right near the tip of the thing's head. If it had possessed eyes, he'd have fired at those, but it didn't. The skin of its head looked just like the surface of the rest of its body, the same light brown as the sand dunes with only slight ripples on its hide.

Tufkakes pulled out his daggers and hit the thing again. "I guess this is its back. Gotta love the extra damage from backstab."

The worm bucked, but somehow Tufkakes and the wolf held tight. It was down to a quarter health.

Baladara hit it hard with a huge fireball, then dropped to her knees. "Man. Cover me for a second. I need a potion." She pulled out a vial and downed it.

Horc glanced at the party icons. Baladara's health was fine, but her mana was drained and slowly coming back as the potion did its work. He continued his slower, more concentrated arrows. They damaged the thing a lot more than anything other than Tufkake's attacks to the back of its head.

Baladara stood and she and Greensleeves managed to get off good solid shots. The worm's health bar started flashing orange.

"A few more shots, guys. We've almost got this." He let fly another Flaming Impact arrow as Tufkakes scored another round of blows.

The beast's health bar flashed red right before the final attack from Baladara and Greensleeves. The worm shivered, then dropped to the sand.

A gold aura surrounded Baladara and she cheered. "Level twenty. About damned time."

A similar aura surrounded Greensleeves. "I guess you don't want to hear level twenty-two."

"Not right now, no." Baladara sat in the sand and pulled out her flask.

"Gotta hand it to these bigger, badder critters, they *are* worth more," Tufkakes said as he set about looting the worm. "Hey Horc, you might want to skin this thing. Might help you advance your profession."

Horc walked over to where the Rogue was working on the worm. "Good point." As soon as his coin purse chimed with loot, Horc pulled out his skinning knife and set to work. The worm was a lot like the snakes had been to skin but was a lot larger. He was thankful the game was just using bag slots and not weight. He had to struggle a bit to get the skin into his bag but felt like it was a pretty good haul. He'd find out when they got to the next vendor and he could sell it.

"Okay, that might have been worth it," Baladara said as she stood and walked over to the cooling carcass. "According to my display, this thing's got some rare alchemical supplies in its gut. Leveling and rare crafting ingredients—yeah, that might be worth hard fights."

"Tell you what—next time, you can get up close and personal with the big bad monsters," Tufkakes said. "In case you've never played one before, Rogues aren't supposed to be front-line fighters. We need tanks."

"That's who we're going after," Horc said as he cleaned his skinning blade off in the sand. "I don't think any of us like having to go close quarters with these things." He reached in his bag and pulled out a big chunk of meat for his wolf before he cast his healing spell. The wolf had taken the brunt of the worm's attack and his health bar was down into the orange. Horc felt bad about not noticing that before. Sometimes there was just so much going on and he forgot things like that.

"Good." Tufkakes cleaned his blades before they disappeared into his belt and other places on his person. "The sooner we get the tanks back, the better I'll feel about everything. I can get all sneaky and just backstab like a good Rogue's supposed to."

"You're doing a good job of that so far," Greensleeves said. "Okay, I checked my map, and it looks like there's a city not far away. Dustbinnia. It's a neutral city, so none of us will have trouble getting in. We can sell a bit of stuff and see if we can figure out which way we need to go from there."

"Sounds good." Horc stood and dusted off his leather pants. "Let's try to remember to look around for an enchanter and see if we can bargain to get my axe re-enchanted."

"I guess you didn't do that in Red Wind Terrace," Baladara said. "I thought that was on the list for there."

"It was, but I forgot." Horc hated having things like that slip his mind, but it was something he was prone to doing.

"All right. Let's see if we can get there without having to kill too many more of these things." Tufkakes looked at Greensleeves. "Which way are we going?"

"That way." Greensleeves pointed off to the right, slightly away from the direction they'd been heading.

"Then that way it is," Horc said. With each step he took, he did his best to be aware of any kind of movement in the ground under him. As the party's Ranger, he should've been the one to warm them of things like worms exploding out of the sand. A Rogue was supposed to warn of traps, not ambushes.

9

BY THE time they reached the gates of Dustbinnia, Horc's arms hurt from the nearly constant fighting they'd endured. The Dunedivers had badgered them at nearly every sand dune they went over or around. But he had become fairly good at detecting their movements moments before they showed themselves, and the party was getting practiced at taking them out, even if the worms were a major battle each time. Horc had added to his levels and walked through the gates at level twenty-one. Tufkakes was level twenty-one, too, which irritated Baladara for some reason.

The morning sun was already heating up the sands. As they entered the town, the temperature dropped dramatically.

Horc glanced around. The adobe buildings all looked nearly the same. It was a larger settlement than Tragiczan had been, but not as large as either Red Wind Terrace or Stone Helm City. "Okay, why the cool down?"

"Maybe a spell of some sort," Baladara suggested, also glancing around. "But I'm not going to complain."

Greensleeves frowned. "And you shouldn't. Theoretically since you're just using VR helmet and gloves, you shouldn't experience the heat like we were. I mean, damn. I'm from the South, and I know heat. People can say dry heat is easier to deal with than wet heat, but that was just a bit much."

"I'm with you there," Tufkakes agreed, wiping his brow. "Luckily, or unluckily, Procyans don't sweat. And I think panting is a bit undignified."

Horc wiped his own brow and was ready to find somewhere with a bit of air conditioning but didn't want to say that and come across as a whiner.

"Okay, quick stop at a vendor to unload stuff, then we're off toward the coast," Greensleeves said. "Hopefully things'll be cooler when we reach it."

"We might want to find ways to protect ourselves from the sun," Horc suggested. A lot of the people around them seemed to be wrapped up in what he would call 'classic desert attire,' with long flowing robes and head wraps to keep the sun off their skin. Some of them were so wrapped up, the only visible parts were their eyes. He figured that made life harder, but if it kept the person cooler, it might be worth trying out. "How much farther is it to the coast?"

Greensleeves got the look that told Horc he was checking something in his interface. "Still a couple of hours. We're almost three quarters of the way from Tragiczan, but Rick was driving us."

"Let's just hope there's a road so we don't have to deal with those damned worms," Tufkakes muttered. "Hey, I bet there's a vendor over there." He pointed to a large open area where people were setting up tents like they were prepping a morning market.

"I wonder if there's an armor, or weapon merchant, and barring that we'll need to find the local smithy," Baladara said. "'Cause I could use a bit of repairs; some of those worms scored some good hits on me."

Horc checked the status of his armor. It was fairly good. Since finding the ever-full quiver, he didn't need to worry about getting arrows like he had just starting out, but his axe had a couple of new nicks in the edge he'd like to get ground out. "Let's not forget the enchanter too."

"Right. It would be nice if that axe did cool stuff again," said Greensleeves as he and Tufkakes led them toward the closest tent.

The heavy robes made it impossible to identify all the various species around the makeshift market, but from their various sizes and shapes, Horc was fairly sure there were more species there than in any of the other towns he'd been in. There were only a few players, and he wondered if others were having trouble getting across the desert. Nearly everyone he spotted was an NPC. He knew that most players followed various quest chains to new locations in a game world. He wondered if other players just hadn't gotten quests out that way, or if for some reason, they were being led somewhere by the game AI. But that didn't make a lot of sense. Game AIs were there to make sure things went smoothly and that the NPCs acted the way they were supposed to. He didn't like the idea of being led around by an AI; that made it sound creepy.

IN THE market, they managed to take care of everything, except finding an enchanter. They did get a lead on that, and Horc led the way as they went down a flight of curving stone stairs into an underground chamber.

At the bottom of the stairs, a heavy wooden door blocked their path. There were no obvious hinges to show them how to open the door.

"Let me look at that," Tufkakes pushed past Horc and the wolf to run his hands along the edges of the door. He pursed his lips and hummed. "Okay, step back."

They all did as he said and he studied the floor.

"This is odd." Tufkakes rubbed his chin.

"What?" Horc asked. He really hoped they hadn't reached a dead end and were going to have to go back to the market to get another lead.

"It really looks like the door just disappears when it's opened." Tufkakes pointed at the floor. "The dust isn't disturbed in any perceptible pattern that I can see."

"Maybe it's a pocket door," Baladara suggested. "We just need to find the right direction to push it, and it slides open."

Not wanting to waste more time than they had to. Horc stepped behind Tufkakes and knocked on the door. "Or we could try knocking and see if anyone answers."

Tufkakes huffed. "And where's the fun in that?"

Seconds later the door slid up into the ceiling with a soft whoosh.

"Well, I guess that explains why there aren't any scuff marks on the floor." Greensleeves pushed Tufkakes and Baladara toward the opening.

Before they could get through, a light blazed bright in the darkness on the other side of the door.

"Stop. What do you want?" A deep voice boomed out of the center of the light.

Horc blinked a couple of times before his eyes adjusted enough he could make out the diminutive figure in a long, light brown robe, standing there with its hands on its hips. The little guy didn't look like he'd be much trouble, but Horc had played enough games to not judge a person's ability to make trouble based on their stature.

"Hello, we're looking for an enchanter, and a vendor in the market sent us here." Horc did his best to sound rough but not pushy. He worried if he came across as weak, the enchanter might jack up his prices, but worried if he was too tough, the guy might not want to deal with them.

"Sent you here, did they?" The little man gave a sly laugh. "There seems to be a good number of you. Are you all in need of my services, or just one?"

"Just one of us," Horc said. "Me. I have an axe I need worked on."

The Enchanter huffed. "An axe? Do I look like a blacksmith?"

Horc shook his head and unslung his axe. "No, sir. I've already had the axe sharpened; what I need is to have it re-enchanted." He held the axe out flat in his hands, presenting it to the little man.

"Re-enchanted?" The little man stepped close and peered at the axe. "Ah yes, the Axe of Gnoll King. Not a really powerful weapon, once all its charges are used up. Had one in each crystal didn't it?"

"That's it exactly." Horc nodded.

The Enchanter turned away. "Nothing I can do for you. Gnoll work is shoddy. Once it's used up, the crystals aren't stable enough to recharge. Now if Dwarves had made the weapon, then it could be revived. You don't happen to have any Dwarven weapons on you, do you?" He turned back and studied the group for a moment. "No, nothing of Dwarven make. Elven, Human, and"—his eyes widened and seemed to glow in the soft shadow of his robe's hood—"a Procyan Death Dagger. Very nice piece."

Tufkakes glared at the Enchanter. "Nobody touches my dagger. It's a family heirloom."

The Enchanter waved him off. "It's always very hard to get a Procyan to part with their weapons, particularly Procyan Thieves."

"I'm a Rogue, not a Thief." Tufkakes puffed his chest out and stood straight.

"Semantics." The Enchanter turned and started walking into the light. "There is nothing I can do for you unless you come back with a better weapon."

Horc was torn about what to do. He wanted to pursue the little man and demand a better answer but doubted that would help. The Enchanter was an NPC, and the odds of physical violence accomplishing anything were minimal. Not to mention that IRL he wasn't prone to beating people up to get them to do things for him.

He sighed. "Well, I guess this was a waste of time. Let's hit the trail and find our way to the coast and see what we can do about locating Steelmaiden and Slasher."

"Are you giving in too easy?" Tufkakes asked.

"Not exactly," Horc said and marched up the stairs, hoping the next time they needed to get information out of an NPC it would go easier. The thing was that Halfworld had already proved that there weren't many things that went easily in the game.

10

THE ROAD leading from Dustbinnia to the coast was made of hard-packed sand and about as wide as a horse-drawn card A fair number of NPC travelers were trudging down the way, coming from the coast with wagons of fish, cloth, salt, and other goods, obviously bound for Dustbinnia and beyond.

"I think this is the most sign of trade I've seen in the game," Horc said as the party stepped off the road to let a cart laden with sturdy barrels go past.

"Yeah, it's like they're rolling out a lot of updates while we're in here playing," Tufkakes agreed, turning to watch the wagon as it continued on its way. "I wonder what's in those barrels and how hard it would be to pinch one."

"Since they don't register when we study them, impossible to tell unless we actually get our hands on one," Baladara replied. "Which I don't want to take the time to do. We need to catch up to Slasher and Steelmaiden and see what's going on."

"Do you guys actually know them IRL?" Tufkakes turned and they all continued walking down the road, which was a lot easier than going through some of the deeper sand that lay a few feet off its edge.

"No. Well, we know Slasher's one of the big wigs in the LA office," Horc said, resisting the urge to stop and get the sand out of his boots. "Steelmaiden's from the Dublin office, so we've never met either."

"But we're wasting all this time trying to get to them." Tufkakes shook his head. "Doesn't really make sense."

Horc took a deep breath. When he stopped and thought about it, there did seem to be a slight flaw in their logic, except he wasn't about to leave their friends, in game or not, to whatever fate they were suffering, if they were suffering, and he had no way to know one way or the other. "They've been standing by me while I'm stuck in this game. I don't think Steelmaiden's logged out at all. I know Slasher did talk with his wife and made arrangements at the office. We can tell something's wrong on the server, so I owe it to them to be there for them like they've been here for me."

Tufkakes looked at the road and rubbed his big pointed ear for a moment. "You're a good man, Horc. Not many people would worry about others like this. Most would say it's just a game and they'll be able to log out at some point."

Greensleeves shook his head. "That's the point. They might not be able to, at least not without help. Something's up with the AI. We need to find them and see what's going on, then maybe we can figure out what Rick and the other developers need to do to get them back to right."

"Besides, they're both in pods, not just VR gear. They'll be having a lot more pain due to that. For all we know they're being tortured," Baladara chimed in. "I don't know if Horc bothered to tell you, but the motto of this group is, 'Friends don't leave friends to die in a dungeon.' They might not be in a dungeon—"

"That we know of," Horc added.

Baladara shot him a dark look. "I was going to say that. But they're obviously in a predicament, and we need to find them. If it's too much for you, then we can let you go from the party and you can chase down that wagon to see what's in the barrels and then figure out where you can pawn your loot."

Tufkakes shook his head. "No. I really think I lucked out when I failed to pick Horc's pocket. You guys are a good bunch of people. I actually wish I knew you all in real life. You'd be good friends."

It felt like he jabbed a knife in Horc's gut. Sure, he had a couple of people from work, like Mike— Baladara—who he hung out with from time to time, but there weren't any he was really close with. Most of his friends were in games, but because of the way his favorite game Galactic Explorers worked, he didn't *need* to make friends there either. He might not want to have a partner or roommate underfoot, but sometimes it might be nice to be able to sit around and enjoy the company of people the way he was doing in Halfworld. He knew if he wasn't having so much fun, he'd be worried to death about what was going on with the pod and his life hanging in the balance. When they got out of the game, he wanted to hang out with Mike more, and maybe he'd make an effort to travel a bit and meet everyone else IRL.

"I like to think we'd be good friends outside of the game too," Greensleeves added with a smile.

"Okay, when we get out of here, we get Total Immersion Systems to pay for all of us to have a luxury vacation somewhere," Baladara quipped. "How about Disney? We can hang out and have real life adventures too."

"We'd have to bring the families if we did something like that," Greensleeves said as they topped a rise and looked out onto even more rolling desert dunes.

"Not if we tell them it's a corporate thing," Baladara said. "Don't get me wrong, I love Lisa, and I wouldn't be suggesting this if she wasn't asleep right now, but sometimes I need more down time from her and the kids than just escaping into a game."

"You didn't tell us that she's watching everything we do," Horc said, suddenly feeling a little awkward at having a voyeur observing everything they did. Then when he thought more about that, he realized that the company had Miranda, their occasional guide and tech support agent, and Rick, and probably a whole lot more people paying attention to everything they did to make sure he didn't get himself killed by accident.

Baladara shrugged. "Since I'm still on gear, I've got everything routed to the main viewscreen in the living room so she can enjoy too. She's not big into playing games, but she really gets into some of the graphics and likes watching me play. Every so often she wants to drive and I let her, as long as it's not during something important."

"You know that's a little weird sounding," Tufkakes said. "If my kids were still at home and watching me play, I'd get majorly uncomfortable. But then if the kids were still home, I never would've been able to afford the pod, or been able to put it in one of their bedrooms." He grinned mischievously.

"A wife is a lot more intimate than kids are," Baladara said. "I'm not sure I'd want my kids to watch me killing rabbits, squirrels, and wolves."

"You had a rabbit quest too?" Tufkakes asked.

Baladara shook her head. "Nope. We started off with pigs. The squirrels were just to help get more points. Horc didn't want to do the squirrels."

"Too easy and just seemed a bit too redneck to just run around killing sweet little innocent squirrels." Horc still didn't like the idea of attacking things that didn't come at him first or didn't have red letters above their heads.

Greensleeves started laughing. "Dude, you don't know squirrels IRL, do you. Nothing sweet or innocent about them. Total varmints. But I'm with you. I can't handle just whacking them as I walk along. I like bigger, stronger prey."

Tufkakes shook his head again. "You guys aren't like most of the gamers I've met and that's a good thing."

Horc smiled to himself as they continued to hike along the road. They'd been lucky and fallen in with a good group. He hoped Slasher and Steelmaiden were okay. Even if he didn't know them IRL, they had quickly become friends.

COCONUT SPRINGS waited for them as they topped the last dune and spotted the coast, a lot closer than they'd been expecting. The seaport was only slightly larger than Tragiczan had been. There were a number of tents and huts that seemed to circle out from where the docks met the beach. But before the party could get there, they had to traverse a long winding trail down a fairly steep cliff.

"I think someone needs to explain geography to the game designers," Tufkakes said as they worked their way down the steep switchback. "If this was real life, I don't think many of those wagons would be getting up the hill. Way too steep. Haven't they heard about coastal plains? Sure, there are sea-side cliffs, but this is a bit extreme."

"Maybe if they built a bigger beach, the town could be larger," Horc said, as he noticed the number of smaller dwellings that seemed to come out of the face of the cliff. He wondered how far into the cliff the city went and wished he would have time to explore it.

"Or that right there might be a reason to keep everything small." Greensleeves pointed toward the ocean. A huge dorsal fin rose out of the water, it was easily fifty or sixty feet tall.

"Is that a shark or a whale of some kind?" Horc peered, but from just the fin, couldn't tell for sure.

Greensleeves shook his head. "Don't know. Extremely large for either."

"Doesn't have a tail following it," Baladara said as she shielded her eyes and peered across the small harbor. "Probably a whale of some sort."

Horc turned from the water and stared at her. "And how do you know that?"

Baladara lowered her hand and shrugged. "Don't remember exactly, probably one of the cartoons my kids are always watching. Lots of strange facts thrown around on those things and you never know if it's right or wrong."

"And since this is a game, it could be either," Tufkakes finished for her. "I just know I'm not swimming in that water. No way, no how."

"I agree." Horc shook his head and resumed trudging down the slope. "I've seen one-too-many giant shark movies to even think about swimming. Hopefully we can find a boat to wherever it is we need to go."

"When we get back to flattish ground, I'll check with Rick and see if he can pinpoint us a local," Greensleeves said, trailing Horc.

"We're going to have to do something nice for him when we get out of this game," Horc said. "Since the wiki is still crap, he's our lifeline." Horc hated wandering around with little idea of where they were going. He was so used to established games that had full wikis and, in some cases entire books dedicated to how to play the game, Halfworld was proving to be a challenge in finding their way around and knowing what to expect from things like dungeons. He was trying to do his part and add to the wiki when he got a chance in hopes of helping other players out.

"When we hit the beach, let's empty bags while Greensleeves is checking in," Baladara suggested. "That way we're ready to roll once we know where we're going, and what it's going to take to get there."

"You two go find the vendors. I'll stay here with Greensleeves while he checks with Rick." Horc waved the other two toward town.

Without another word, Baladara and Tufkakes headed on through the tents and huts.

"Thanks for hanging back with me," Greensleeves said as he walked off the path and leaned up against the granite cliff they'd just made it down. "I'll just be a couple of minutes."

"No problem." Horc leaned next to Greensleeves. "The wolf and I will be right here."

As if responding to Horc talking about him, Horc's wolf companion came over, sat in front of him and whined.

"What's up, boy?" Horc asked and glanced at the wolf's health bar, just to make sure he didn't need to be fed.

The wolf pushed his head into Horc's hand, just like a real dog would.

Horc grinned and stroked the wolf's head. "You really are just like a real wolf, aren't you? It's really cool how much detail they put into you. I can't just keep thinking of you as a wolf, from now on, you're Wolf. I know it's unoriginal, but hey, I've never had a pet IRL and that's just easy for now."

A chill went through Horc as the green text over his companion's head changed to Wolf. The AI was listening to him, or maybe because he was talking to Wolf, he was talking to it too. He shook off the feeling and for several minutes stood there, stroking the wolf's head, while a couple of wagons reached the base of the cliff and started up the winding incline. The NPC drivers shouted at their horses and oxen, driving the animals hard to get to the top of the cliff.

"Okay." Greensleeves straightened and blinked. "They seem to have been stationary for a while now. Looks like they're on an island due west of here." He pointed out past where the creature with the gigantic fin was still patrolling the harbor. "We're going to need to get a boat. Rick said if he wasn't in the middle of a major discussion with the other programmers about the AI errors, he'd come and give us another ride."

"Wait a minute—" Horc's pulse raced. "Errors? As in more than one?"

Nodding, Greensleeves headed toward the pier. "Yeah. Seems our two party members aren't the only players missing in the game. Since it's just partied people who are reporting a problem, the game designers aren't sure if there are more people affected or not."

"This doesn't sound good," Horc followed Greensleeves, trying to remember where he'd seen Baladara and Tufkakes disappear to. It had been into a hut past the last tent. If there were people disappearing in the game, that could spell major trouble for Total Immersion Systems if anything bad happened to them.

"It's not. Rick's going to try to give us what help he can, but right now, it's all developers on deck to try to get this sorted out." Greensleeves pointed to where Baladara stood in front of a hut. "There they are."

"Okay." Horc followed him over. There weren't the crowds of people, both NPCs and players they'd encountered in some of the other cities, but Coconut Springs wasn't that large either. Horc tried to pay attention to the people around him but didn't see any players at all. When he stopped and thought about it, he hadn't seen any players since Dustbinnia and worried they'd wandered too far from the areas other players had already been in. Somehow being the first to explore a place didn't make him feel that wonderful, not when they still weren't sure he'd survive if he died.

"So, what'd you find out?" Baladara asked as they drew close enough to hear her.

"We're looking for a boat to Lone Palm Arena," Greensleeves replied. "They've been static there for some time now."

"Lone Palm Arena?" Tufkakes came out of the hut, wiping his hands and grinning. "Doesn't sound like a really friendly place."

"It's an arena, and it shouldn't even be open to players yet," Greensleeves said. "I think that's part of what's got Rick and the others worried. Sure, there are NPCs there, and there are boats from several places, including Coconut Springs, but so far, no players have received quests to go there."

"So, there's no reason for Slasher and Steelmaiden to be there," Horc surmised.

"Right. Something odd is definitely up, and if we're going to find out what it is, we're going to need to go there." Greensleeves looked past Baladara. "Give us a minute to go in and empty our bags and we'll be ready to find a boat."

"Tell you what, why don't we go figure out where the boat leaves from while you two take care of your stuff?" Tufkakes offered. "Shouldn't take you too long, as long as you don't get him too confused."

Horc stared at the Rogue. "Too confused?"

Tufkakes took Baladara's arm. "You'll see."

Deep lines crossed Baldara's face, and she just shrugged. "See you two on the pier."

"I really hope Tufkakes didn't do anything to this vendor," Greensleeves said quietly as they entered the thatch hut by pushing a red, heavy, sand-covered blanket to the side.

Horc followed close behind with his wolf at his heels. "I wonder if things like that are going to be one of the hazards to having a Rogue in the party."

"Depends on how well it's played." Greensleeves didn't say anything else as he walked over and woke the Goblin clerk up. He was pretty deeply asleep and Greensleeves had to pinch his long green ear to get a response out of him. Once he was awake, he dealt with them quickly and they left the shop in a couple of minutes.

Horc couldn't shake the feeling that Tufkakes had done something to the little green man but had no proof. It didn't make sense that the shopkeeper had fallen asleep so quickly after the other two party members had finished dealing with him, unless there was something affecting his program too. If there were major problems in the game, that might make it harder than ever for Horc to stay alive and he didn't want to put his friends under too much stress helping him do that.

11

THE ROLLING of the boat across the waves hit Horc hard. If there was one thing he never expected to get in a game, it was seasick. The *Dancing Mermaid* had timed its escape from Coconut Springs Harbor when the thing attached to the big fin was at the greatest distance from the dock.

The ship was a large schooner. Its holds weren't big enough for much in the way of cargo, but the captain, an obnoxious Goblin with one eye and a peg leg, named Captain Calamity Kidd, promised she was a fast ship, and had made the run to the Lone Palm Arena many times.

Horc walked up on the bridge and waited while the captain finished dressing down a battered-looking Gnome who had apparently not swabbed the deck correctly and let water build up in a spot that was already showing signs of beginning to rot.

As the Gnome hurried off carrying a mop, Horc closed the distance to the captain. "Could I ask you a question?"

"Depends." Kidd didn't look at him, apparently keeping his attention on the ocean around them.

"On what?" Horc wasn't in the mood for word games. He was hoping the captain might have some answers for them.

"What kind of question it is." Kidd slowly shook his head. "I can't tell things that were told to me in confidence, I'm sure you understand that."

Horc forced back a sigh and leaned against the thick wooden railing that encircled the deck. "You said when we boarded that you've made this run many times. Are you the only boat that goes from Coconut Springs to Lone Palm Arena?"

Kidd nodded slowly, not taking his gaze off the ocean ahead of them. "That's true. But then, we tend to run with just one boat from point A to point B. Saves on confusion. Why do you ask, Ranger Horc?"

"We're looking for some friends. They appear to have been kidnapped from Tragiczan and taken to the arena, or at least, that's what our sources say. I was wondering if you might've seen them."

"I've ferried a good number of people across the ocean to that destination. What do your friends look like?" He still kept his focus on the sea and acted like he wasn't really talking to Horc.

"A big Warrior named Slasher and a Barbarian woman named Steelmaiden." The way the captain was acting, he wasn't about to provide Horc the information he needed, but Horc didn't feel like it would hurt to ask.

"Hmmm." The captain finally looked away from the horizon and at Horc. "Yes, I think there might have been a Warrior and a Barbarian in a group seeking passage a day or so ago."

"A group? An adventuring group, or a different type?" It was a lead they were on the right path.

A message flashed on his screen.

Quest Completed: Snuff out the Darkness
Follow the trail of darkness and find out where it leads.
Rewards:
5,000 XP

A small thrill went through Horc as his XP bar flashed and filled in. It had been a while since he'd had any indication he was one the right path to make progress on the quest as well as work toward finding Slasher and Steelmaiden.

His screen flashed again.

Quest: Snuff out the Darkness
Stay on the trail of darkness and reach the end.
Rewards:
5,000 XP
Accept - Decline

"Accept," Horc whispered.

Kidd stared at him, then laughed. "Not sure what you're on about, but adventurers don't travel to the arena, yet. At least not of their own free will. Just remember, you're on the seas here, laddie. Even traveling with an experienced captain like myself doesn't necessarily ensure a safe ride."

For a second, Horc wondered if he was getting threatened, then one of the crewmen shouted. "Fogbank off the port bow!"

Captain Kidd frowned and turned the direction the crewman indicated. "There shouldn't be a fogbank that far from shore. All hands, on deck!"

Around them crew members appeared from every hatch and ladder. Baladara, Tufkakes, and Greensleeves ran up from the berths they'd been in.

"What's going on?" Baladara asked.

"Fogbank." Horc pointed in the direction of the thick clouds rolling toward them. "But the captain did confirm that Steelmaiden and Slasher were here, but not of their own free will."

Greensleeves peered across the horizon. "That's not good. I can't believe the AI's kidnapping players. I bet there's a boat in that fogbank." His hands started glowing light blue as he worked a spell. "This one's new, but it should work out here, better than some," He thrust his hands forward and a jet of wind curled the waves opposite from the way they'd been rolling moments before.

The only sign of the wind's passage was the movement of the waves. When the wind hit the clouds, they splashed up like waves hitting a breaker. The clouds swirled around but didn't break.

"Magic!" Captain Kidd shouted. "The pirates'll be upon us in no time. Battle stations!"

"What can we do?" Horc asked, hoping the captain wouldn't try to dance around that answer with something stupid like…'what can you do?'

"Help my men repel boarders." The captain spun the wheel, and the *Dancing Mermaid* changed course, running parallel to the clouds instead of toward them like it had been.

The ship's altered course seemed to encourage the pirates in the cloud. The mass of darkness churned like an angry storm as it rushed toward them, swinging slightly as if it was trying to cut them off at the pass, or whatever the nautical term was for such a maneuver.

"Don't start anything until they drop their clouds, or come on board," said the captain, as he spun the wheel again, cut hard back in the direction they'd been going, and heading right across the path of the clouds.

"I might be able to Shadowwalk over there," Tufkakes said. "I don't know how far I can go, but if they get close enough, maybe I can get over there and do some damage to them before they do any damage to us. That would be good."

"Yes, it would," Horc agreed. "But don't risk too much. If we're going to be boarded, it might be just as well to stay here and hit them hard once they come over."

Baladara pursed her lips and sighed. "You know, I've never done a sea battle in a game before, or IRL either for that matter. Sure, I've seen them in movies and such."

"But this is too close to real life," Greensleeves finished for her. "I'm with you. But hey, at least it appears to be a random encounter and will add something to an otherwise boring voyage."

"If you say so," Horc said. He wasn't sure if he should try his arrows, or if his axe was going to be the more effective weapon for close-quarters fighting on the ship. At his side, Wolf tensed and growled as the clouds brushed the schooner's edge.

"Brace yourselves!" the captain shouted.

Something inside the cloud bumped the *Dancing Mermaid*. Three heavy grappling hooks came out of the clouds and dug into the wooden rails on the ship's side.

"I'll be back." Tufkakes stepped backwards into the shadow cast on the deck by the ship's sails. He fuzzed out a bit, like a television channel having trouble holding onto a signal, then he was gone.

"Okay, if I haven't said it before, that's freaky," Baladara said as she started a spell making her hands glow red. "Let's see how these pirates like a fireball in their sails."

"If you can hit their sails," Greensleeves said as his own hands glowed with the light blue of an air spell.

Their spells passed through the first layer of clouds that had blocked Greensleeves' earlier spell. After a couple of seconds, there was a small explosion, and flames engulfed the clouds. The gray and white wisp flared red, then faded away. In the wake of the clouds a huge ship with dark sails towered over the smaller schooner. A large number of pirates of a multitude of species glared down at them.

Horc's heart sank. They'd managed to sail into a huge mess that he wasn't likely to be able to survive, but he was damned if he was going to just lay down his bow and surrender. He pulled an Impact arrow from his quiver and after casting Flame on it, loosed it up at the nearest pirate. Around him, the rest of the *Dancing Mermaid*'s crew were also firing what ranged weapons they had.

From under the deck, something exploded and the pirate ship rocked back away from them, only the grappling hooks held it tight.

"Someone get those damned hooks out of my boat!" Kidd roared at the top of his lungs.

Two of the crew ran to the hooks and started pulling at them. Shots rang out from the pirate ship. Bullets and arrows hit the *Mermaid*'s deck and the men fell back, one of them clutching his side while his health bar dropped.

Horc forced himself to focus on the pirates above them. He didn't have the time to worry about the NPC crew. Firing multiple arrows, he forced a couple of pirates away from the rail, but there were many more there waiting to take their places. Even the ones felled by Baladara's spells were quickly replaced with fresh attackers.

"This is the biggest mob we've faced so far," Baladara said as she got off another spell. "Greensleeves, grab my pack and start pulling out potions, we're going to need them."

"On it." Greensleeves said after his own Druid spell left his fingers.

Horc got off another couple rounds of arrows before the pirates grew bold enough to start coming over the railing, heading toward the *Mermaid*'s deck. With shouts and taunts, the pirates leapt from their ship into the schooner's rigging and onto her deck. The effect made Horc want to drop his weapons and dive into the water. They looked like huge ants swarming over a carcass, ready to pick it clean.

He didn't have time to pick his targets, he fired at every dark-clad body that didn't look familiar. Within several shots in a row, he was out of mana and relying on the special arrows in his quiver, thankful for the quiver's enchantment that let him always have arrows. A pirate attack would be a very bad time to run out of arrows.

"Horc, you focus on our boarders, I'll keep firing on their ship," Baladara said. "I don't want to set our sails on fire."

"Roger that," Horc said and realized he should probably not risk Flame arrows when his mana came back up and stuck with Poison.

"Here." Greensleeves thrust an open vial into Horc's hand. "Mana."

"Thanks." Horc slammed the vial's contents back then resumed firing. Every shot rewarded him with a scream and a thud as the pirates fell from the rigging. The ones who weren't killed between his shot and their fall, quickly fell to Wolf's fangs and claws. Most of the pirates were level 15 or 16, fairly easy, and would be no contest if they were dealing with them in a one-on-one combat, but what they lacked in base power, they made up for in numbers. It was only going to be a matter of time before one or more of them broke through their assault and got close enough to do some damage to one of the party, or worse yet the captain. Horc knew he didn't know how to pilot a schooner; if it had been a starship in Galactic Explorers, he wouldn't have had a problem, but the schooner didn't have a computer willing to help him make the hard-steering choices and things like that.

When Wolf yelped loudly, Horc glanced over and realized his companion was facing down three pirates on his own. He quickly targeted and fired, sending multiple Razor arrows to finish off the men Wolf had already injured. Red flashed in the corner of his screen and Wolf's health was dropping fast. Pausing in his arrow barrage, Horc cast his Healing spell to renew Wolf until he could feed it. As soon as the spell left his fingers and Wolf's health bar was back in the green, Horc resumed his firing.

Something bellowed, then a huge fur-covered ball flew from the pirate ship and hurled toward the deck of the *Mermaid*. Its landing shook the schooner hard. Then the ball uncurled and a towering pirate covered in thick white hair with huge cutlasses in each hand glowered at them.

"A Yeti Pirate?" Baladara screamed.

"Too hairy for me," Greensleeves said, then hit the brute with a brown blast of Druid magic.

Horc wanted to add his arrows to the fight with the big man that looked to be more beast than pirate, but if he did, then they'd be overrun with the more manageable boarding party members.

"Damn it!" Baladara yelled.

When Horc looked over, the massive pirate had grabbed hold of her. She was trying to cast spells directly into its face, but it kept shaking her before she could get the spells off. Physical attacks were one of the ways to break a mage's casting, and it seemed to be working on Baladara.

Before Horc could get a target lock on the Yeti, it smashed Baladara hard into the deck. Her health bar flashed red, then went out.

"No!" Horc shouted and fired arrows as quickly as he could into the big beast.

"Let me help," Tufkakes shimmered into existence in the shadow of the pirate ship. Seeming to have appeared while in motion, the Rogue flung himself at the big pirate's back and drove a dagger deep as Horc got off another round of multiple arrows at the pirates trying to avoid Wolf's attacks. He wanted the Yeti to fall for what it had done to his friend, but didn't want to risk being overwhelmed by the rest of the mob that was doing its best to swarm them.

The big pirate screamed in pain from Tufkakes' knives as it stepped over Baladara's fading form and reached up toward Captain Kidd. The Goblin danced out of its way and slashed at it with his sword.

Horc risked turning his attention away for an Impact arrow shot, hoping the arrow's slowing spell would help give the defenders a chance to get the upper hand on the humongous pirate.

As he turned back to the pirates still pouring over the side of the ship, he realized their numbers were dwindling. When his mana dropped again, he just relied on special arrows, knowing Greensleeves was busy helping take down the largest pirate.

A glow flashed on Horc's screen.

Level Twenty-Two

The icons around the rest of the party also flashed.

Horc glanced over where the others were standing over the body of the Yeti. Then went back to hitting the last of the pirates coming over the side. "You guys might lend me a bit of a hand here."

"Oh, yeah, we might." Tufkakes used the shadows along the deck to almost dance among the pirates, quickly dealing lethal blows to each one before going on to the next. Within moments the boarding party was defeated and they were able to stop and assess the damages.

I'm back guys. Well sorta. Baladara

Where are you? Horc asked quickly, glancing around to see if he could spot her. He wasn't sure where she'd respawn since they were at sea. He was thankful it was a game and not real life. If she'd taken that kind of damage IRL, she'd be dead. Even if she'd been in a pod, she'd most likely feel battered for a day or so due to the feedback the pods provided.

Lone Palm Area Graveyard Baladara

Sit and rest up if you can. We beat the pirates and will be there in a little while. Greensleeves.

Will do. Baladara

"You are a party of incredible warriors," Captain Kidd said, wrapping a piece of cloth around his arm as a makeshift bandage.

"We do our best," Greensleeves said, bending down to search the Yeti for loot. "This big guy must've been the pirate boss."

"Nope." Tufkakes shook his head. "The pirate captain is dead at his steering wheel. I managed to take that fool out fairly easily. The Yeti was the first mate and I guess, when I killed their captain, he figured he'd return the favor by trying to off ours. Too bad we're better than they are."

Horc tossed Wolf a chunk of meat and bent to loot the nearest pirate, a small Gnome with chipped teeth that had one of his arrows in it. When he looted the Gnome Pirate, his coin purse clinked with loot. As they hurried to loot all the bodies on the deck before they disappeared, Horc tried to stay focused, but there were so many different types of pirates dead on the boards. Gnomes and Goblins were on and under the bodies of Humans, Elves, and even a Procyan.

"I wonder if these pirates were here by choice, or if they'd been conscripted." Horc was reaching for one of the first bodies to fall as it vanished. "Crap. Hurry up and loot, guys. They're starting to vanish." He scrambled to get to the next one before it returned to the electrons that had spawned it.

"Don't worry about them," Tufkakes said. "There's more than enough on the ship to keep us all very happy for a long time."

"And which one of us is going to claim the ship?" Greensleeves asked.

Horc straightened and stared at the big pirate ship. "What do you mean claim the ship? Isn't it just going to fade back into the system like these guys are doing?"

"Probably not," Tufkakes said. "If you look up at the top of the mast, it's got a loot symbol up there. That means that whoever defeats the pirates gets their ship."

Horc stared and at the top of the mast was a spinning golden dollar sign, the game symbol for something that could be looted. Normally it was small enough he didn't always make out the actual sign, but on the ship, it was proportionally huge. "Wow, so that thing belongs to one of us?"

"Or it could belong to all of us, if we'd formed a guild already." Tufkakes said. "Not sure we could do that out here."

"Probably not," Greensleeves said. "But let me check on something." He got that faraway look that said he was checking in with Rick on the question.

Greensleeves blinked after a minute. "Sorry. Rick can't set that up. We're going to have to get to a town to do it ourselves. But the good thing about that is we'll be able to think of an awesome guild name."

"But what about the pirate ship?" Tufkakes wondered. "We're going to have to do something with that before we get back to a large enough town to find a guild master to handle our setup."

"Let Horc hold onto it," Greensleeves suggested. "He's the reason we've all partied together. When we get to a big town and can find someone with enough gold to buy it, he'll be the one to divvy up the goods for us."

Horc wasn't sure exactly what it was going to take to claim the ship as loot, but he was willing to try. The gold from such a prize would set their toons up nicely for a long time. "Okay. How do I do this?"

Tufkakes looked from the ship to Horc and back again. "I'd say go over on the ship and focus on the main mast. There should be a window popup like when you claim a soul-bound item asking you if you want it."

"Okay. I guess I should hurry or it might disappear while we're flapping our gums over here." Horc instructed Wolf to stay as he grabbed hold of one of the ropes attached to the grappling hooks and climbed up to the deck of the pirate ship. Halfway up, he realized there was no way he'd be able to do that IRL. He was in decent shape, but not that good. Climbing rope was never his thing.

Once on deck, he headed over to the main mast of the ship. There wasn't any kind of glow around it or anything that indicated he could select it. He tried waving his hand at it. Nothing. He tried touching it. Nothing.

"Clock's ticking over there," Tufkakes shouted from the schooner.

"Working on it." Horc had never tried to claim anything that large in a game before. When he'd bought the *Star Reacher* in Galactic Explorers he'd just gone to a ship merchant, shelled out his credits, the ship appeared in his inventory, but he'd had to go to the docking ring of the station to use the ship from his inventory.

Horc glanced around the deck trying to spot anything with a glow. The steering wheel shimmered with a gold light. He dashed up to the piloting deck and touched the wheel. The gold light turned red and a message appeared

You do not possess the skills to use this item.

Do you wish to claim it anyway?

Yes - No

"Yes." Horc muttered.

The ship shook under his feet, then disappeared. There was a heavy clinking in his coin pouch as he fell feet-first into the ocean.

Salt water filled his mouth as he swam up toward the surface. He was instantly thankful for the swimming lessons he'd endured as a kid. He'd have hated to drown in the ocean after he'd just survived a pirate attack.

"Did you get it?" Tufkakes shouted as soon as he surfaced.

Treading water, Horc quickly looked at his inventory. The pirate ship was there, with a thin red line around it. He'd seen similar lines around weapons he couldn't use, but the weapons hadn't asked him he wanted them or not. That message must've been due to the nature of the boat. "Yeah. I got it."

"Wahoo!" Tufkakes cheered. "We're rich! You guys are awesome to hang out with."

Horc resumed paddling toward the schooner as Greensleeves and Tufkakes lowered a rope ladder for him to climb back up on. Although he'd never expected to fight pirates, it had been rather fun, other than Baladara dying, but she was fine and already at their destination. If they were lucky, they'd make it to the island without any other mishaps. But the loot from the pirates had been sweet.

12

HORC STOOD in the bow of the *Dancing Mermaid* as the schooner approached the island where the Lone Palm Arena was. Baladara had kept them appraised of what she was finding, which was a fair number of players, most of whom appeared to be in chains, or practicing for some kind of gladiatorial competition. It sounded fairly bleak, but so far, she hadn't spotted either Steelmaiden or Slasher.

"It doesn't look to be a large island," Horc said as he studied the windblown beach at the base of the pier with its single palm tree that grew near a high stone wall that appeared to run at least halfway around the island. "How hard is it going to be to find them?"

"Depends on how much of the place is underground," Greensleeves replied. "The thing with game world construction is the designers aren't always limited to what the natural world allows. Sure, according to Rick, they tried to stick to as Earth-like as possible with Halfworld, but they did take some liberties."

"Some?" Tufkakes laughed beside them. "Come on guys, I'm a walking talking raccoon, that's more than some liberties."

"And possibly going deep underground on an island is another one," Greensleeves agreed. "The other problem, is Rick's having trouble figuring out which designer team worked on this island, so he can find us information on it."

Horc stared at the Druid. "Wait, what? How can they not know who made this island? What kind of design team are they running if they can't figure out who did what?"

"Rick's freaking out about it too, although he's trying to hide it." Greensleeves frowned and gestured to the rapidly approaching dock. "This island is showing on their maps, but there are no details, and no one knows how it got there. There's no paper trail for it. It's almost like the game put it there for some reason."

"I don't like this." Horc shook his head. "The more I hear, the more it sounds like the AI running the game knows more about what's going on than the people who designed it. That can't be good."

"And it's not how it's supposed to work," Greensleeves agreed. "Remember, I'm not the designer in the family, but from what Rick's saying, there's been more than just this instance where there are abnormalities in the game play. Things they didn't design in. The big problem is until we can get you out of the game, they can't take it down. Well, now we've got to get other people where they can log out too."

Horc nodded. "Right, so we ride this out until we can get everyone safe, then they take things down and figure out what's going on. My big question with all this is why wasn't this discovered before we began beta testing?"

Greensleeves shrugged. "Can't answer that one. Again, not the programmer. If I come back and say that the AI may have been waiting for an opportunity to take over, it comes across as paranoid and giving the program a bit too much sentience."

"Our robot overlords are just waiting for the chance to take control." Tufkakes glanced up at the bridge where Captain Kidd was steering them closer to the pier. "Do you think we need to help tie this boat to the dock?"

"Most of the rest of his crew was lost in the battle with the pirates," Horc said, realizing they hadn't seen but a couple of the schooner's NPC crew since the battle that had left Baladara dead only to respawn on the island.

"Is he going to wait for us, or will he keep on his preprogrammed pattern and go back and forth between here and the mainland until we're waiting for him to pick us back up?" Tufkakes asked.

"Wow, don't know," Greensleeves said. "But I bet we won't be able to break his pattern, particularly if the AI is acting up."

"Then we better get ready to disembark," Horc said as the schooner pulled up alongside the pier.

Baladara appeared at end of the wooden planks, like she'd been standing there the whole time. "Well, come on, you guys, before the ship starts off again. If this game's like most, he's not going to wait around for you to get off."

Horc looked up at the Goblin captain. "Thanks for the ride! I guess we'll catch you on the return trip."

"I'll be back later." Captain Kidd raised a hand in parting. "Hope I can find a replacement crew quickly."

"Good luck." Horc turned and followed the others off the boat, a strange feeling of dread settling into his stomach as he went. He just hoped the boat would be there when they needed it. If they had to make a fast escape from the island, not having the boat there would make things a lot harder.

Wolf seemed happy to see Baladara standing at the end of the pier and raced back and forth between the Elven Mage and Horc. He woofed more dog-like than wolf-like and wagged his bushy gray tail.

"You know, I really think he's become more and more pet-like," Baladara said as she rubbed his head.

"Could be," Horc agreed. He hadn't wanted to say anything since he didn't want to make it sound like he was normalizing his companion. The thing was, Wolf was become a lot more than he had been at the start, and Horc wasn't sure what that meant.

"Well, have you found out anything more since your last check in?" Greensleeves asked as they strolled down the dock toward the light brown sand of the beach.

Baladara shook her head. "Not really." She pointed to the wall. "I didn't say anything about the wall because I don't think it's really important, although looking at it from this angle, it's probably meant to defend from pirates or other people attacking from the pier. But it doesn't go all the way around the island. At the one edge I went around, it looks fairly unfinished."

Horc frowned. He wasn't sure he liked the idea of an unfinished wall. If the AI was building the island from its own imagination, they might be in real trouble if they got trapped on the wrong side of it.

"Let's check out the other end," Greensleeves suggested. "Since you've already been the other way. Maybe we'll find something more useful."

"This way then." Baladara headed off to the left.

"So where were you seeing them practicing for gladiatorial stuff?" Tufkakes asked as they walked across the sand.

"Not far from the respawn spot in the graveyard. It's almost like they tried to make the spot as convenient to the arena as possible." Baladara paused and stared out at the ocean. "Oh, that doesn't look good."

Horc turned and followed her gaze. Several large serpent men were swimming quickly toward shore. The low hanging evening sun glistened off their blueish scales and sharp tridents. "Definitely not good." He stared at them until they were close enough he could make out the red text over their heads, indicating their hostility. **Serpent Cult Warrior, Level 25**, read the first one.

"There's at least six of them," Greensleeves said. "They look like they're coming this way."

"Why are we already pulling agro?" Tufkakes asked just as Horc's screen flashed red, indicating something had targeted him.

"No clue." Horc pulled his bow and knocked an Impact arrow. "But I'm not waiting for them to hit us first." He added Flame to the arrow and let it fly at the closest warrior's blue-scaled head.

"With you there." Baladara let fly a Fireball at the same snakeman. The two attacks hit the thing in the head. He reeled backward as his health dropped nearly half of what it had been before they hit it.

"Hard and fast guys," Horc said as he hit the thing again.

As the others started their attacks, Horc focused his arrows on one warrior at a time until they fell. By the time he was working on his second target, they were reaching the beach and Wolf was able to lend his fangs and claws to the assault on them.

Being on the beach seemed to empower Greensleeves' new, sand-based spells. Torrents of dirt and small shells lashed out at the snakemen who were advancing on them.

"This is really weird," Baladara said as she got off another fireball and started a magical force blast. "There weren't any of these things around the other side of the island. I wonder where these guys came from."

"Different side of the island, different rules?" Tufkakes threw two daggers at a reptilian warrior closing on Baladara, drawing its wrath on himself.

"Possible," Greensleeves' sand attack finished off the Warrior he and Horc had been working on. "Or maybe we're being viewed as more of a threat."

"I hope not," Horc said as he targeted the snakeman slithering quickly down the beach toward Tufkakes. "Having the AI viewing us as a threat wouldn't be a good thing, particularly since I'm not supposed to die in the game at the moment."

"Trust me, even if you were, it's not a great experience," Baladara said as she got off another blast of magical force and her mana began flashing orange. "Damn these things are taking a lot out of me right now."

"Hold on." Greensleeves pulled out a potion and tossed it to her. "Use this."

Tufkakes threw himself at the one rushing him. The move seemed to take the reptile by surprise and the Rogue managed to get on its back. His blades flashed in the dying sunlight, and quickly ended the thing's life.

A huge form rose up out of the surf, easily twice the size of the other Warriors. There were still two of the original set they were having to deal with.

Snake Cult High Priest, Level 28.

"Guys take these others out, while I keep the big guy off you!" Horc pulled an Impact arrow and gave it a Poison spell. He knew the others could knock out the lower level ones if he could keep the big guy off their back, but to do that, he was going to need to hit it with Impact arrows to slow its movement and keep it slow until they could help him bring it down. Wolf turned its attention on the High Priest as the first arrow struck.

The snakeman slowed but the word **immune** flashed in red letters on Horc's screen.

"He's immune to poison." Horc used Flame on the next arrow. His manna flashed red. He wasn't going to be able to cast spells on his arrows quickly unless he got a potion, and if he took time to down a potion at that moment, it might give the High Priest the opening he needed to close in and do major damage.

"We're almost done here!" Greensleeves said.

As Horc glanced at the party icons, he used a Razor arrow. Greensleeves was holding pretty well, but

Baladara was again low on mana, and Tufkakes was below half health. The snake cultists were taking a toll.

Horc got off another Impact arrow just as the High Priest shook off the effects of the first one. Even with the damage from the arrows and Wolf, the big reptile was down only a quarter of his health as it slashed at Wolf with its huge trident. "Get potioned up first." Horc hoped he'd have the opportunity to get a mana potion when the party was able to distract the High Priest from him.

"Working on it." Greensleeves threw a couple of potions to the others as he started casting a healing spell.

"Good." Horc back up, trying to keep the High Priest in bow range so he wouldn't have to go melee with it. He stumbled on something buried in the beach sand.

"Shit." He went down hard on his back, dropping his bow.

The High Priest broke out of the Impact arrow's slowing effect and surged at him, even as Wolf grabbed its tail and bit down hard. The snake man threw its trident at Horc, who managed to roll out of the way just in time.

Surging to his feet, Horc pulled out his ax. The High Priest still had over half of its health, and its hands were suddenly moving in rapid movements and glowing with a blue glow Horc recognized as a healing spell.

"Oh no you don't." Horc rushed the reptile, swinging his ax down on the thing's hands as hard as he could. He didn't want to risk the chance that it could regenerate part, or all of its health and make it that much harder to kill.

When his ax hit the serpentman's hands, something exploded. The force of the blast knocked Horc back several feet into the sand. His health flashed, and he lost a quarter of his points instantly. Pain shot through his back. His ax was gone. He still held the handle, but the blade was obliterated.

"Damn you, Ranger!" The High Priest rushed him looking like he was ready to pummel Horc with the sparking, bleeding stumps of his hands. Its health was approaching a quarter, but it was still up and fighting.

"What just happened?" Horc scrambled to get back on his feet. With his ax destroyed, he reached into his quiver for arrows. He might not be able to fire them, but he could hopefully slash at the monster with them.

"You made boom." Tufkakes jumped on the High Priest and drove a knife into the base of its skull.

Horc jammed a Razor arrow into the thing's chest.

The High Priest screamed as its health flashed red, then went out. It collapsed onto the sand.

"Well that sucks." Horc pulled his arrow out of the scaly chest, wiped it off in the sand, and returned it to his quiver. "Guess that ax is really done for now."

"Kinda looks that way," Greensleeves said as he began casting a healing spell on Horc. "I guess a disenchanted weapon isn't the best thing to use to break a casting, huh? We'll have to remember that if we ever have another weapon that loses its magic."

As the spell finished, Horc's health returned to full. "I guess we'll just have to make a point to keep away from Gnoll weapons in the future."

"But you managed to blow that thing's hands right off." Baladara stood from looting the one of the other corpses as coins jingled in everyone's purses. "That was really impressive."

"And gross," Tufkakes said. "You did see that thing dripping blood as it rushed him."

"Yeah. That was cool too." Baladara brushed sand off her hands. "Don't be such a girl about things."

Tufkakes frowned. "You don't have to be a guy about everything. We could try harder to do more role playing here."

"Maybe when the stakes aren't so high," Greensleeves said. "Now, let's see about getting off this beach before more of these things show up. This wall can't be that much longer, can it?"

Horc dusted himself off and remembered to toss food to Wolf, who'd sustained a bit of damage in the fight. "I hope not, but we don't know what we're going to find over there either. It might be worse than this."

Baladara shrugged. "When I was watching, it wasn't too bad, if you don't mind watching other players obviously being enslaved by whatever the AI is up to."

"Then we'd better be careful." Horc wasn't sure how smart it was for them to go venturing into somewhere if the AI was working against them in more ways than just as a game master trying to make the story interesting to the players. It was like going against some kind of all-knowing deity who'd gone on a kidnapping spree and was determined to keep everyone it got its hands on. He was already a prisoner of the game in a different sense, and just hoped things weren't going to get worse.

13

HORC HURLED the handle of his axe into the ocean as far as he could. "Well that cheap thing is gone. The only problem is now, I don't have a melee weapon."

"Hold on a second." Tufkakes opened his bag and started digging through it. "I think I've got something in there. You can use a sword, right?"

"Sure." Horc stood off to the side and watched Tufkakes. He didn't normally have trouble digging through his bags. Normally he opened up his bag, thoughts about what he needed, and it appeared in his hands. He wondered whether this digging that Tufkakes was going through was some kind of negative thing for Procyans. He knew most races and classes had both positive and negative traits. Tufkakes had said something about some major buffs Procyans Rogues received, and it made him wonder if digging through bags was a debuff of some sort.

After a moment, Tufkakes pulled out a long sword. "Here. It's too big for me. I'm limited to daggers and short swords."

Horc looked at the sword.

Katana of Cutting

Damage 27,

Speed 17

"It's nothing special, but it's close to what that ax could do." Tufkakes held the sword out to Horc.

Taking the sword, Horc turned it over in his hands it felt fairly light. "A little less damage than the axe did, but it's a faster weapon."

"So, if the battle lasts long enough, you'll get in a couple of extra blows." Baladara looked at the sword. "Overall not a bad exchange, and it's definitely better than trying to just stab people with arrows."

"And if we're lucky we can get some better drops." Greensleeves frowned. "I'm guessing it doesn't have a sheath."

Tufkakes shook his head. "Asking for a lot out of random drops, aren't you?"

"Yeah, sometimes it would be nice if the game made things a little easier." Greensleeves started walking down the beach the way they'd been going.

"No worries, I can just tuck it across my back for now." Horc slipped the sword into the strap he'd been carrying the ax on. It felt different, but easier as it settled there. At least with the sword, he wouldn't feel like he was missing something if the fights got into close quarters.

THE WALL ended a short distance farther down the beach. The opening was uneven, with the base sticking out farther than the top, and the way it looked, it would be easy for someone of average build, or smaller to simply walk up the end and then walk along the top of the stones. Since they hadn't met any resistance other than the Serpent Cult dudes, Horc was fairly sure the wall wasn't officially finished, but that made him wonder why the AI hadn't just willed the wall into existence complete, without flaws. There were a lot of things in Halfworld that didn't make a lot of sense to him.

"Does this feel too easy to everyone else?" Tufkakes asked.

Baladara shrugged as she waved them all to stop at the end of the wall. "Yes and no. That's what I was thinking when I found the other end of the wall and did a bit of scouting. Honestly, there doesn't seem to be a lot of guards around, but then all the players I stumbled across were already captured by the pirates, so I guess a lack of security makes sense. There are some wandering guards as we get closer to the arena proper, and the bad guys I spotted were all triple-X level, so all we know is they're more than we really want to take on."

"Which isn't a good thing." Greensleeves peered around the rocks. "We need to figure out how this whole place works and what we're going to need to do to free Steelmaiden and Slasher."

"And any of the other players who've been caught up in this mess," Horc added. He hated the idea that other players were being held by a malfunctioning AI. He didn't know a whole lot about how AIs functioned, but he was fairly sure they weren't supposed to hold players hostage. Sure, in Galactic Explorers, he'd played scenarios where he had to rescue other players, but that had always been during special events and if the party wasn't rescued within a certain amount of time they were allowed to log out and then resume the game at the point right before they'd been captured for the special event.

"If we can," Tufkakes muttered. "You know more than a few of these guys are complete assholes."

"Yeah, we know," Greensleeves muttered with a sigh. "But nobody deserves to be stuck in a game long term."

"It's hard enough knowing I'll get out eventually as long as I don't die here. They probably don't know that." Horc looked over Greensleeves' shoulder, not seeing anything important, or any other people nearby. He wondered how many of the players caught by the AI had freaked out when they realized they couldn't log out. He'd had his own freak-out moment when he'd heard a tornado had hit his house and he was stuck in his pod. It hadn't been a long one. He wasn't prone to major freak outs, but in the back of his mind, he was still worried something might happen and he'd never be able to return to his body and eventually his mind would disintegrate into the ether of his pixel-prison.

"Exactly." Greensleeves turned away from the wall. "So how do we want to handle this?"

"We need to get in there and find out what's going on," Baladara said. "I can slip in using an invisibility spell, but that only covers me."

"I can Shadowwalk in," Tufkakes suggested. "But again, it doesn't help more than just me."

Horc looked between them. "I don't like splitting the party—that's how we got in this mess to begin with."

Greensleeves shrugged. "We might not have much of an option. You, Wolf, and I can't be that sneaky. If we try to go in with them, we'll all probably get caught."

"Sometimes we have to split the party," Baladara said. "Besides, odds are, Steelmaiden and Slasher didn't know what they were getting into."

"You don't either," Horc countered. None of them knew what to expect, particularly if the AI had gone rogue. There was too much of a chance something would go horribly wrong and things would get much worse. They were playing a game. None of them expected things to become life or death. In games, if people died, they simply rezzed at their respawn site and kept going.

"Right, but we have a much better idea," Baladara continued. "I bet they'd do it for any of us… if they could."

"She's got a point," Greensleeves said. "Besides, we never know how much information they'll be able to dig up while they're in there. Also, if they can get in and out fairly easily, or at least in a way they can remember, then we'll be able to communicate with Steelmaiden and Slasher while we're working on getting them out."

There was no way Horc could argue against that logic. They desperately needed more info to be able to make informed decisions. "Okay. Fine. You two head in there. Be careful."

They both flashed a thumbs-up.

"We'll be back." Baladara's hands moved and quickly vanished, followed by the rest of her.

"Show off." Tufkakes stepped back into the wall's shadow and slowly faded from view.

Horc watched him disappear and hoped the knot in his stomach was just basic fear that he wasn't going to see his friends again. There was a good chance nothing was going to happen to them and they'd return shortly with news they'd found their missing party members and even had a plan to get them out.

"Why don't we go hang out by those palm trees over there?" Greensleeves pointed to a small clump of tall, slender trees not far away. "They aren't much but will give us a little bit of cover."

"Better than hanging out here waiting for someone to spot us peering around the edge of the wall." Horc glanced down at Wolf sitting next to him. "Come on, boy, let's get out of the direct line of sight."

"And there's shade over there," Greensleeves added. "Not used to sweating in the game yet. It's almost too real."

Horc nodded. "Yeah." There was a lot about Halfworld that was more real than he'd been expecting, but he knew the pod was adding to their experience. The more he could just enjoy the sensory experience and forget about his own life or death concerns, the more he could enjoy the game that went beyond things he was used to playing.

As they reached the palms, the air in front of them shimmered like a heat wave and Miranda appeared. She looked the same as she had before in her long gray robes and short brown bob. The only thing missing from her previous visions was her tall staff. She still didn't have any text over her head.

"Well, at least, you're trying to stay alive this time," she said, turning slightly as if to get a look at their surroundings.

"Yeah, we are," Horc said. "Have you got any news? Is my pod free?"

"They are about to pull the plug on your pod at the house and hook it into a portable UPS. Since I'm your sys-admin, and just got promoted to pod system director, I'm here to make sure there aren't any problems on this end when that happens. The backup battery on your pod is nearly depleted so they reached you just in time."

Horc frowned. "Nearly depleted? I thought those things had a two-week life-span. At least that's what we tell the customers."

Miranda shrugged. "You've been doing tech support long enough to know that what we tell the customer and reality is often two different things."

Fear lanced through Horc. If the rescue team had been slower to reach him, his body might've died while he'd been in the game doing god-knows-what. "Now isn't the time to drop bombshells like that."

"Right," Greensleeves stood at Horc's side glaring. "I haven't been able to find any data that suggests less than two weeks."

"And to this point, we haven't had anyone really test the system long term. There was no reason for it." Miranda got a faraway look. "Okay. Alan, let us know if you feel anything strange."

"Anything like—" Pain lanced through him. Cutting off his words. Horc tried not to but couldn't keep from screaming at the top of his lungs. His entire body was on fire and felt like he was being torn apart. He couldn't think about anything else but the heat in his veins. It shot out of him, racing from his core like he was a volcano trying to explode.

Then as suddenly as it started, the pain stopped. Horc dropped to the ground, panting.

Greensleeves put a hand on his shoulder. "Dude, are you okay?'

Horc took a long centering breath. "Maybe. Damn, I thought I was being torn apart while being set on fire from the inside. That's not something I want to do again." He wiped a hand across his brow, and flung sweat onto the light brown sand he was sitting in.

"But you survived," Miranda said. "That's a good sign. Do you have a Log-Out, or Exit Game option?"

Bringing up his main interface, Horc quickly scanned the options. He shook his head. "Nope. Exit Game is still grayed out."

Miranda pursed her lips, put her hands behind her back and started to pace. "We were hoping that when we reset your power connection, you might get more of a system reset. It didn't happen. We're going to have to do some more digging and see what we can figure out. Until then, keep playing a smart game and stay out of trouble."

"We're playing a game. We shouldn't have to be staying out of trouble." It was all Horc could do to keep the irritation out of his voice and not snap at the woman. Things were making less and less sense the longer he was stuck in the game.

"You're an anomaly in a game that shouldn't have any." Miranda replied. "One of several anomalies right now. We've got to do what we can to keep you safe. You know that." She stared at Greensleeves. "David, you know this. Rick should've told you all about this. See what you can do to keep him safe." Without another word, she vanished.

"Wow." Horc stared at the spot where she'd been. "I didn't think she could get any more annoying, but it looked like I was wrong."

"Some of the sys-admins are like that," Greensleeves agreed. "I guess I should be happy Rick isn't."

"Which brings up the question of, why he isn't our contact?" Horc started to stand, but his head swam, so he opted to stay seated on the warm brown sand.

"I guess she's out of the Dallas office." Greensleeves offered Horc a hand up. "But if she just got a promotion, I would think she'd be more valuable elsewhere, unless they're thinking a senior pod person should be handling your situation personally.

Horc shook his head, figuring he probably had time to sit there for a little while before Tufkakes and Baladara returned. Maybe by then he wouldn't be so wobbly from them changing out his power source. "There's a certain logic in that. She must be working directly with the rescue team." If changing out the power supply had hurt as much as it had, he wasn't sure he wanted to experience what would happen if his uninterruptable power supply was somehow disrupted. He suddenly felt safer with his pod trapped under the rubble of his house as opposed to in some transport driving to a Total Immersion Systems lab where they'd begin trying to get him out of the pod and back to the real world.

14

SOMETHING RUMBLED in the distance. It sounded like bricks being slapped together. The sand on the beach shimmied with each impact.

Horc looked around. "Okay, what was that?"

"Not sure." Greensleeves stood from where he'd been relaxing against one of the palm trees. "Want to go check it out?"

"Sure." Horc wasn't sure. There was so much going on in Halfworld that he was quickly getting to the point he didn't want to check out strange sounds for the fear that they might finally find something that was beyond their ability to successfully confront. When he'd been in so much pain; as they'd finally gotten to his pod and disconnected it from his near-failing UPS, it made him realize how much danger he was in. It was more than a game. For him, it might be life or death. He didn't want to die in the game, because of the game, or even because of the damned tornado that had leveled his subdivision. There was a lot he still wanted to do with his life. But sitting there in the grove of digital palm trees on a beach where the sand was no more than pixels, he couldn't think of any of the important things. He knew there had to be more to life than sitting in a cubicle all day long and putting himself into his gaming pod at night, but it was eluding him. He didn't want a family, he knew that. He wasn't a family sort of guy. He liked going out with friends, although he didn't do that nearly enough. There were adventures to be had in the real world.

As he and Wolf followed Greensleeves out of the grove toward the sound that was shaking the game, he glanced down at Wolf. He'd never had a dog IRL but wondered what it would really be like to have something, someone dependent on him, but was willing to give unconditional love. He scratched Wolf's ear as they walked. It might be nice to find out. He wanted out of the game. He wanted to have a chance to live his life more fully than he'd been living it. There had to be more.

"Well, that's not good." Greensleeves stopped and pointed to the wall.

Horc stared. The wall was building itself. Brick by brick the wall was growing taller and longer, curving around the island's edge. "Baladara didn't say anything about the wall growing."

"And we didn't see any evidence of it on the edge we went around." Greensleeves said as a rough block appeared out of thin air and dropped several inches down onto the layer of blocks below it. A sharp crack rolled across the beach. There was a loud screech as the block slid a few inches, so it bumped up against the previous one dropped on its row.

"Maybe when she was around the other side it wasn't building for some reason and it's trying to reach the edge we went around." Horc shook his head. "The other question, if it's the AI that's building the wall, why not just create it whole, why go to the trouble of making it block by block? That doesn't make a lot of sense."

Greensleeves stood there on the beach, looking thoughtful. "Yes and no. I'm not a coding expert, that's Rick's job. But what if the AI doesn't know the codes for creating a finished wall from scratch, what if the codes it knows are for blocks and it figured out that blocks make a wall."

"So, it's learning." Horc scratched his head as another block appeared out of thin air and dropped onto the wall with a loud clack. "AIs are supposed to do that, but I'm not sure I like the idea that the AI running the game I'm playing is learning how to kidnap players and build walls. That really can't be good."

Greensleeves nodded. "I agree. Let's get back to the grove and I'll let Rick know about this. They can't do much about the AI until we can get you and everyone else out safely, but they can at least start planning."

"Getting everyone out safely is a great idea." Horc wasn't about to leave anyone in the game, particularly those who couldn't log out, players stuck like he was.

"Your pain when they changed out your power supply shook you up, didn't it?" Greensleeves asked as they turned and started back toward the grove of palms where the others would know to look for them.

Horc shrugged. "I guess it did. Until then, I knew there was a chance something might go wrong, and I might die, but the pain… Greensleeves… David… you have no idea. I've never felt anything like that in real life and I never want to feel anything like that again. It was horrible."

"It looked and sounded horrible." Greensleeves stopped and put his hand on Horc's shoulder. "Alan, you can't give up hope. I know Rick and the other programmers are working hard to make sure you get out safely. We have to trust in them to do their jobs and make things right."

Horc nodded. "I know. After that pain…" He shrugged and shook his head. "I don't know. Something changed. I realized that if something went wrong, I really could die in here and there's so much I haven't accomplished in life."

"What are you missing?" Greensleeves put his arm across Horc's shoulder and steered him along the beach. "You don't have kids or a wife, or partner. Do you want those things?"

"No. Geez, it's not that. Maybe I want to find a way to leave a mark on the world. I'm the lead on a tech support team. That's not a mark on the world. It's not like there aren't tons of people out there who could do my job. Hell, Mike could do my job and probably better than I do."

"Then what do you like doing in your off time? Who is Alan Gosling?"

Horc kicked at the sand as they walked. "Maybe that's the core of the problem. I'm thirty-four years old and have no idea who I am. There has to be more to life than just tech support and video games."

"I like to think there is. Rick and I like going down to the beach once in a while." Greensleeves pointed with his free hand out to the gently rolling ocean that stretched out across the horizon. "Of course, it's not as quiet and unpopulated as this one. There're still waves and sand, but there's lots of people." He sighed. "Okay, come to think of it, that's just escaping life, isn't it? We play games like this together. We occasionally go out with friends…" He sighed again. "Okay, this probably isn't a great time to get to thinking how pathetic my life is, it's not going to help you."

His admission brought a chuckle to Horc. "Yeah, we don't both need to get down in here. We can work things out once we get out of here…or when I get out of here. You're not stuck. You can leave at any time."

"Not that long ago, we would've said that about Slasher and Steelmaiden too, now they're stuck."

The palm grove appeared around the next turn of the island.

"There is that," Horc agreed. "This game is as fluid as life can be. We all need to watch out what's happening around us and stick together."

"Right." Greensleeves gave Horc's shoulder a final squeeze and let go. "Nice to have gotten our brains thinking. We just have to stay focused."

"Hey!" Baladara shouted, jumped and waved from near the trees.

"Looks like they made it back," Greensleeves said. "Let's see what they found."

Horc nodded, getting back into the action would help him out. It would make things easier, taking his mind off his problems, both in the game and outside of it.

It took them a couple of minutes to reach the trees. When they got there, there was just Tufkakes and Baladara. They were leaning against the trees, looking tired.

"Did you find them?" Horc asked as they entered the grove.

"Yeah, that was the easy part," Baladara replied.

"So, we're not going to be able to get them out?" Horc didn't like the sound of that. Even in his case the techs were saying he'd be able to get out of the game, they just had to figure out the right way to do it.

"We're going to have to work something out," Tufkakes said. "Their cells are protected by some kind of magic that is either keyed to players, or too high a level for us to be able to disrupt."

"Leveling might be harder without them." Greensleeves put his hands behind his back and paced around the sand.

"Honestly, I'm not that worried about leveling as getting them out," Baladara said. "We don't know how long people in pods can last." She looked at Horc. "So far you've been lucky. Your power supply is holding out. What happens when that gives out? Even those fancy uninterruptable supplies run out of power at some point. Two weeks is what we tell most people."

"And mine hadn't been going as long as that and was nearly gone when the rescuers reached me." Horc almost forgot she and Tufkakes had headed out before Miranda showed up and he'd endured the change of power supplies.

"You're out?" Baladara's face lit up. "That's awesome."

Horc shook his head. "No. They got the pod out of the basement. The plugging in the new USP nearly killed me in game…well no damage exactly, but it hurt like hell. They're taking it to a facility where they can hopefully work out what went wrong."

"Ah, man, that sucks," Tufkakes and Baladara said at the same time.

Pointing between them Horc raised an eyebrow. "Okay, so what's up with you two? Having similar thoughts now? I wouldn't have expected that."

Baladara shrugged. "Let's just say we had a little bonding during our side journey and leave it at that. Tufkakes is cool."

"And so are you." Tufkakes punched Baladara in the shoulder hard enough to make her take a step to the side and then rub her upper arm.

"Okay, so now that we're caught up, what are we going to do?" Horc asked. In the distance the sound of the bricks falling on the wall grew louder. "The wall's getting closer."

"Wall's getting closer?" Baladara put a hand over her brow and stared into the distance. "Is that what we're hearing?"

Horc nodded. "Yeah. Bricks are appearing out of thin air as the AI builds the wall."

"Okay then, we need to get on the inside of the wall." Baladara looked around. "It sounds like they're going to start having arena games with their people and players…their people meaning the kidnapped folks and from what Steelmaiden said, animals too."

"It might be a way to put on some levels while we're here and would give us the opportunity to stay on the island while not attracting too much attention to ourselves," Tufkakes added. "We can probably work out a plan better that way too. If we have to take out the bad guys, having a plan always works better than not."

"Right." Horc really hoped things weren't going to get to the point they were going to have to run for it, with or without the rest of their party, but as Tufkakes and Baladara laid out what they'd discovered, it sounded more and more like they needed to be ready to run at a moment's notice. That wasn't good, but they had to save their friends.

15

ALTHOUGH THEY made sure to cut along the inside of the wall, they walked around until they found the gate. After a brief discussion, they decided it was probably safest for them to stay on the inside of the wall, so that if they *couldn't* find a gate, they could still be close to rescue Steelmaiden and Slasher, once they had a plan.

"We definitely need to apply to fight," Baladara suggested. "That way nobody thinks it's weird that we're hanging around."

"You don't think they're going to have spectators at these arena games?" Horc asked, not really sure if he wanted to put his name into the hat for those people fighting in the arena. There was a lot of possibility for accidents, or worse yet, death in such games. If the pirates were as ruthless as Baladara and Tufkakes claimed, they could be in for a real problem.

"Not this early in the game," Greensleeves said. "Odds are they aren't going to have many players wanting to fight either, although there's sure to be some. A lot of players love Player Versus Player combat, they live for PVP."

"Being able to beat up other player and not suffer a penalty for it gets them off," Tufkakes added.

"That's right." Baladara agreed. "Odds are those folks will be swarming the place as soon as word gets out."

"Then, we're better off finding a way to get the others out quickly before those guys start showing up," Horc muttered. He didn't like the idea of beating up on other players. His thing was having adventures in games. He liked having adventures. Maybe he needed to be finding ways to have them in real life. He patted Wolf as they walked up to the gate. It might be nice to have adventures he could take a dog on. It could be a lot of fun.

"There is that." Greensleeves turned and pointed. "Let's start there."

Just inside the gate was a small hut with a window cut into the thin wooden sides. It looked like it was meant to be a ticket booth or something similar. The palm fronds that made up the roof, hung low enough to provide a modicum of shade for the skinny Goblin sitting on the other side of the window with his chin sitting on his green hands.

"Oh, he looks like a real winner," Tufkakes whispered.

"With you there, TK" Baladara said.

Greensleeves waved them off and headed for the hut.

"TK?" Horc asked as they headed after the Druid.

"It's easier to say than Tufkakes." Baladara hurried a little harder than the taller folks.

"I'm okay with it," Tufkakes said. "I might even start calling her Ba."

Baladara shook her head. "B.A. maybe, 'cause I am a bad ass, but not Ba. I ain't no sheep."

Horc rolled his eyes as they reached the hut. It was fairly obvious the two had gotten some major bonding done over the course of their split from him and Greensleeves. He was a little surprised by it; Baladara had sounded fairly anti-Tufkakes at first. But he hoped their bonding wouldn't be short lived and they wouldn't be back at each other's throats in no time.

"So, what do we need to do to sign up for the arena?" Greensleeves was asking the Goblin as Horc walked up to his side.

"The boss didn't say anything about the portals being opened yet. Where are yous guys from?" The Goblin's high voice squeaked slightly as he spoke.

"Red Wind Terrace," Horc said, doing his best to look tough and ornery. "Words out among the Orcs that you've got a major battle arena going here and they sent me to check it out. We didn't use any portals to get here, came by boat."

"Boat. Yeah, I cans see that. There was a boat out by the pier a while ago." The Goblin rubbed his pointed green chin, pulling slightly on the thin verdant goatee growing there. "What took yous all so long to get this far? It ain't like it's very far from there to here."

"Had to stop and fight off those cultists that are hanging out near the dock," Horc replied, hoping he remembered what the aquatic serpent men had been called.

"They're supposed to weed out the weak." The Goblin grinned, showing broken teeth. "But if yous guys made it past them, then yous must be ready for the arena. I'll let the boss know we've got our first contenders. He'll be pleased." The Goblin leaned over the windowsill and frowned. "But we've got a bit of a problem here."

"What's wrong?" Horc's heart sank. Things had seemed to be going really well, but the Goblin didn't seem happy about something. With the NPC leaning toward them, the yellow text over his head was visible.
Bo' Jangle, Goblin, Thug, Level 25

"There's four of yous guys. The arena ain't set up for four players in a team, three or five, not four." Bo' settled back on the stool that raised him up high enough he could see out. "One of yous gotta go."

"What if we only fight in a team of three?" Greensleeves suggested before Horc could say anything. "We won't ever have more than three on the field at one time."

Bo' squinted at them. "So, like one of yous would be an alternate?"

Horc nodded. "Exactly. We promise not to have more than three of us on the field at one time."

For a moment, a thoughtful quirk danced on the corner of Bo's thin lips. "Okay." He pulled out a clipboard from under the windowsill and slid it to them. "I need names, classes, and levels." He seemed to study them for a moment, then pointed at Baladara. "Put the Elf as your alt. Mages don't normally do as well in arena fights as others, particularly low-level Mages. They run out of mana too fast, then dash around screaming to distract the other team."

Baladara frowned and put her hands on her hips. "I wouldn't run around screaming."

"Unless there were rats," Tufkakes said with a grin.

"Unless there were rats," Baladara agreed with a scowl.

Greensleeves took the form and started filling in the spots without saying anything. After a moment, he lifted the quill and looked at the rest of the party, then nodded. "Okay. I think that's it. The form doesn't say if our Ranger will get to have his companion with him or not."

Bo' took the form back, and ran a narrow-pointed finger along the lines of text Greensleeves had filled in. "Looks fine to me. Yeah, yeah, an animal is part of being a Ranger. But by signing up for the arena means you've agreed to the regulations, so yous all will be responsible for cleaning up after him. We find any wolf poop in the sand and there'll be trouble. Understand?"

Horc tried to remember if he'd ever seen Wolf poop or pee. Sure, he ate all the time, but he couldn't remember if anything came out the other end. If that might be a problem in the arena, then he was going to have to keep an eye on things and make sure there wasn't anything left behind.

"Sure, we got it," Horc said.

"Good. Now, give me a couple minutes and I'll show yous to the competitors' quarters where yous can rest, sharpen yous's swords and get ready for yous's matches. Oh yeah." Bo' again leaned across the windowsill. "If any of yous guys has magical weapons of any kind, the arena's magic will block your weapons' spells. We take magical cheating very seriously in the arena." He hopped off the stool and dashed out the back of the hut.

A lump rose in Horc's throat. He might be in big trouble, and it was too late for them to change their minds. The paper had been signed. "Does anyone have any arrows?"

"What are you talking about?" Baladara's eyes grew wide. "Crap. Your quiver. If the arena is going to eliminate any imbedded spells on weapons, you're going to be stuck with one magical arrow from each kind you had in your quiver."

"Exactly." Horc wished they had a better answer. He was going to be stuck using his sword and Wolf to win battles. Then an idea hit him. "Either that, or I'll need a new quiver and a supply of arrows."

"And where are we going to get that?" Baladara asked.

Horc glanced at Tufkakes as Bo' returned, coming through a large wrought iron door in a fence behind the hut. "We've got our Rogue. Maybe he can find something."

"Maybe he can." Tufkakes grinned.

"This way," Bo' waved them toward the gate he'd just came through. "I've got yous the best room in the barracks. The boss is really excited to get going, so yous's first match will be in an hour. He wants to see what yous can do before he risks yous on any of our stronger players."

"Sounds good," Horc said as they turned from the hut and followed Bo' through the fence and toward a low stone building he could only figure was the barracks Bo' mentioned moments before. Stepping through the gate sent a shiver up Horc's spine. It felt like they'd just entered another part of the game, like they were separate from where they had been, but that was ridiculous. If there was something like that, either Baladara, or Tufkakes would've said something. He was just being paranoid.

AFTER BO' left, Horc studied the small room they'd been brought to. It wasn't much to look at. Five narrow wooden beds with straw mattresses and no sheets or pillows, a washbasin, a rickety table with three chairs, and a threadbare rug that looked like it might've been brightly colored when it had been made.

"If this is their best room, I don't think I want to see their worst," Baladara quipped as she sat down on one of the beds, then got right back up again. "Okay, yeah. I have no idea how people used to handle straw mattresses."

"I think we've already seen their worst rooms," Tufkakes said as he started to pace. "Those cells below were definitely worse than this."

"Okay, you've got me there, TK," Baladara agreed. "I wonder if we can get some food, or if we're expected to eat our own."

"Why don't I slip out and see what I can find." Tufkakes walked over and tested the door. "Okay, at least this isn't locked. I'll be back." And he faded away into the shadows. Seconds later the door closed.

A sense of ease washed over Horc. Something deep in his guts unwound. "Why does the door being unlocked make me feel better about this whole thing?"

"It means we aren't prisoners…yet," Greensleeves said.

Wolf hopped up on one of the beds, circled once, laid down, wrapped his tail around his nose and closed his eyes.

"The yet bit doesn't make me feel better about this," Horc muttered as he went and sat on the bed with his companion. The matress was lumpy and thin pieces of straw stuck out of the mattress and into his legs. It was definitely something he wasn't going to take his clothes off to sleep on.

"Okay. Tell you guys what." Baladara stretched and yawned. "If nobody has any objections, I think I'm going to log out for a while and get some real-world rest. You guys are in pods, I'm the only goggles and gloves guy here and my chubby butt is getting worn out."

Greensleeves nodded. "I'm good with it. Since we don't know how long you're going to be, or how long we're going to be here, I'm going to partially log out and check with Rick to see if there's any way he can link your coming and going to Horc. If I'd have thought of that earlier, you wouldn't have had to work so hard to catch up with us at Tragiczan."

"Just don't let me pop back in somewhere in the middle of Red Wind Terrace, or some other zone where the natives will be hostile."

"Good point. If you want to hang out for a few minutes, I'll check with Rick and come back." Greensleeves sat on the bed across from Horc and slid back until he was leaning against the wall. He frowned and shifted to pull a piece of straw out of his pants. "Human druid leathers were definitely thicker and sturdier than the Desert Elf linen pants are." He closed his eyes.

Baladara stared at Greensleeves for a moment, then looked at Horc sitting on the bed petting Wolf. "Okay, so how are you really holding up?"

Horc shrugged. If Baladara had asked earlier, before his talk with Greensleeves, the answer would've been different, but he was feeling better than he had been. "Decent. Not as great as I was, but I'll get through."

"Dude, I've got no idea how you're holding out as well as you are." Baladara resumed the pacing she'd done earlier. "I'd be a total basket case. That incident with the power source swap sounds awful."

Horc nodded, not really wanting to go over it again. "It was bad. I've got to have confidence that we're going to get through this. If I don't I'll fly apart." He took a deep breath. "Do you feel like you've got a good life? In the real world, I mean."

Baladara shrugged. "Wife, kids, mortgage, decent job. It could be a lot worse."

"Yeah, that's true. Do you worry about how you're going to leave a mark on the world?"

"Nope. I've got my kids. You don't have any. Are you beginning to wonder what your life would be like with them? Don't do it, man. I love my kids, don't get me wrong, but don't do it. There's too many people in the world today, that's why we escape to places like this."

"Is that what gaming is to you, an escape?" Horc kept petting Wolf; the simple repetitive motion was more relaxing than he would've thought it could be.

"That's what it's supposed to be for everyone." Baladara sat on the bed next to the one Greensleeves was on. "Gaming helps people deal with the real world. If gives us places to go and things to do that aren't as horrible as the world we live in."

Horc had always thought so when he played science fiction games like Galactic Explorers, but Halfworld seemed like something a lot bigger, a lot more addictive. He wondered how long it was going to be before people started finding ways to stay there until their lives ran out in their pods, and when they reached that point, what would happen to them in game. Would they continue to go on? Would they simply vanish in a puff of pixels? There was a lot science didn't totally understand about the way people interacted with the AIs in a VR world.

"You think our world is horrible?" Once he started asking Baladara about things, Horc really wanted to know the answers.

Baladara pursed her lips and sighed. "Wow, I think I'm way too tired for this kind of talk, but here goes. We're on the verge of destroying Earth. Maybe if we hadn't had the huge science versus religion fight twenty or thirty years ago, we wouldn't be tottering on the brink. If people had taken steps to counter climate change that tornado wouldn't have destroyed your house and killed so many people. If, as a society, we'd embraced space travel, we'd be living on Mars by now and not just settling the third lunar base. Yeah, O'Brien Corp is making major strides in getting some new engines ready to push deeper into the solar system, but we should already be out there. Our cities are overcrowded. The oceans are dying. Even if we could find a way to clean up two hundred years of pollution, we've already lost over three quarters of the species there. So yeah, I think our world sucks. We need things like Halfworld and the other games to give us places to go so that we can remain sane. If it wasn't for the ability to escape into the digital world, I don't know what I would do. There's nothing I can do to fix things now, so all I can do is find ways to keep my brain together."

"Wow, I never knew you felt like this," Horc continued petting Wolf, and wondered if it would be better for him and any pet he had to keep it in the digital world, that way he didn't have to worry about its carbon footprint, feeding it, walking it, and the ramifications of those actions.

"How can any of us with a brain not feel that way? Sure, we spend as many hours as possible away from the real world." Baladara closed her eyes and put her head against the wall. "Lisa and I swap out a lot of the time so there's someone there to watch the kids. She's got this odd dancing game she likes to play with half naked bodybuilders, but sometimes it's furry games, or other cosplay games that are a lot cheaper than real cosplay. But all of it's better than hanging out IRL more than we have to. I don't really care about the mark I'm going to leave on the world as long as I go out decently and leave something to give my kids a chance at a decent life."

"You're making me feel better about not having kids." Horc closed his eyes for a second. "But I don't want to just vanish into the pixels and never have anyone remember who I was. I want to be more than just some guy on the other end of a phone or a chat who was able to help someone figure out how their pod works. Does that make me a bad guy?" Horc kept rubbing Wolf. Each caress helped him relax.

"No, it doesn't make you a bad guy, or girl as the case might be. It makes you human. I just want something more out of life. When I get out of here, I'm going to start looking for something more. I just don't know what it's going to be."

Greensleeves blinked and straightened. "Okay, you two look deep."

Horc waved off the comment. "Don't worry about it. Can Rick help out?"

"Sure. I've sent you his number. Send him a text when you're ready to re-enter the game and he'll check on where we are and land you with us if possible, or nearby." Greensleeves smiled. "I think he's enjoying helping us like this."

Baladara laughed. "So, he likes cheating in games. I like your guy. Okay, I'm out of here for a while. Don't have too much fun without me."

"Will try not to." Horc wondered how many rounds they'd go through in the arena before she came back.

Then Baladara was gone.

Horc stared at the spot where she'd been. She'd logged out before and came back without a problem; he hoped that would happen again. He didn't want to be stuck in the game without his friend.

16

HORC TOOK the quiver and arrows Tufkakes handed him.

"Not much, but it's all I could find. Let's hope the captive armory doesn't notice them missing." Tufkakes ran a hand through his hair. "I did my best to pick something that was behind everything else. The way these pirates are, I really don't want to piss them off until we have to."

Rifling through the arrows, Horc nodded, then frowned. He wasn't going to complain, but there weren't any special arrows in the selection, then he reminded himself that magical arrows wouldn't work in the arena anyway. He wondered if that would also apply to the spells he could cast on his arrows to give them extra punch. "I'll have to make every shot count." He lay the quiver on the bed next to where Wolf was licking his paws.

"We're going to have to be careful with this anyway," Greensleeves said. "There's too much of a chance of something going wrong. Most of the players aren't going to worry about dying since they'll be thinking they can just resurrect in the graveyard near the dock and keep playing. We still don't know about you, and after what you went through with Miranda's last visit we don't want to risk things."

"Right." Horc glanced at the spot in the room where Baladara had vanished. She'd only been gone a short while, but he wished she'd hurry up and finish sleeping IRL and come back to lend a hand. Somehow this logout was hitting harder than the others, even though with the others they'd known less about what was going on.

The door to their room opened and the Goblin, Bo' sauntered in. "Alright guys, the first round is ready for yous." He stopped and glanced around the room. "Hey, where's that useless Elf Mage of yous'?"

"She had to log out for a little while," Greensleeves said first. "She'll be back later. She doesn't have to be here since we can only have three of us fighting at one time, right?"

Bo' nodded rapidly. "Yeah. That's right. Okay, this makes yous guys more legit anyway. Grab yous' stuff and let's get fighting."

Horc grabbed his bow, the quiver Tufkakes had 'found' and his sword. It still felt weird having a sword after using an axe for a while, but he knew with practice he'd get used to it.

Wolf jumped off the bed and followed them out of the room.

"Do yous let that happen at home?" Bo' asked as Greensleeves closed the door and they started down the corridor.

"Let what happen?" Horc asked not exactly sure what the Goblin was on about.

Bo' huffed. "Letting the wolf on the bed. I mean geez, it's a bed. Good people sleep on it. You don't want them to get fleas and such."

"Wolf doesn't have fleas." Horc did his best to sound put out, even though he hadn't stopped to think about his companion having fleas. Could a VR animal have digital parasites?

"You better hope not." Bo' didn't say anything else until they came to the end of the tunnel and stood on the edge of the sand in the arena.

Spreading his arms wide, Bo smiled. "I give to yous, the arena."

Horc scanned the area. It looked much like the Roman arenas depicted in movies he'd seen. The wall running around the outside of the area was a little more than head-high. The sand was tan and perfectly smooth. Above the wall, several tiers of stone seats rose up until they reached another wall. Spaced about halfway around the wall from where they stood there were two mini-towers, he couldn't think of anything else to call them, they rose about another head above the outer wall and were open to allow their occupants a better view of the arena than the lower seats did. The two towers faced each other, as if they were set up for rival kings to decide the fate of their subjects.

The tower to their left had occupants. One of them was a huge man who looked to be at least half Orc, but Horc wasn't sure what the other half was since he was lankier than either Orc or human and his tusks were huge, reaching nearly to his eyebrows. The red text above his head was far enough away Horc had to squint to see it. **Rothand, Level 35 Fighter Pirate Lord.**

"I guess that's the big guy the others mentioned," Tufkakes whispered near Horc's ear.

Horc nodded once. He really didn't want to do anything to piss off the pirate lord. He looked like more than they could take on, easily.

"Yous guys really need to get a group name," Bo' said. "It would make introducing yous a bigger deal. If yous survive this round, give it some thought."

"We will," Horc replied. "Who are we fighting?"

"They'll be out in a minute," Bo' replied. "Let me get out of the way first." The Goblin scampered away, back down the corridor and a heavy iron gate dropped down as soon as he passed its location.

"I guess we shouldn't be too surprised by that," Horc said as the clang of the gate dropping finished ringing out across the arena.

"I guess we don't get to escape until it comes up again." Greensleeves shook out his hands as the gate across the arena from them rolled up.

"Here they come." Tufkakes dropped into a crouch and a pair of knives appeared in his hands.

Horc pulled an arrow and nocked it. He added his Flame spell to it and waited. The arrowhead sizzled next to his finger. It was nice that his magical add-ons were going to work.

A trio of gangly green men bounced into the arena. The red text over their heads read **Hobgoblin Level 24**. Their armor was piecemeal and none of them had a complete outfit. They all had different weapons, one with an axe, one a sword, and one a long spear that looked taller than he was. None of the weapons looked to be in great repair.

"I've got the axe guy," Greensleeves said as a wave of sand rose up at his feet and crashed into the oncoming Hobgoblins, knocking all three back a few steps.

"Swordsman." Tufkakes threw a dagger at the one with the sword.

"Guess that leave us with the spear dude," Horc muttered to Wolf as he focused his attention and shot on the NPC with the polearm. He was thankful that none of their first opponents were players. He wasn't sure he was ready to fight players, even assholes like the mailroom Paladins.

When he let the arrow fly, it was a great hit, taking the Hobgoblin in the right eye. The thing flopped to the ground and then started hitting its face as the flames erupted across its head.

Horc checked his display and saw that the Hobgoblin was already down half its health points. He drew another arrow as Wolf dashed across the sand toward the fighter who was rolling on the sand, doing his best to put out the flames.

THE ARENA

Again, Horc held his arrow, focusing his attention on the Hobgoblin to make the most of the shot as he added as Poison spell to it. This arrow took the gangly beast in the huge dangly left ear for another critical hit. It stopped moving and lay on the sand. Somewhere nearby a gong rang out.

Horc glanced up, half expecting to see a scoreboard showing their team ahead, but there wasn't anything obvious.

Pulling another arrow, Horc glanced around to see who needed help. Greensleeves' health looked to be down farther than Tufkakes. His opponent was only down a quarter of health too.

Focusing on the Hobgoblin with axe, Horc unleashed his arrow, adding Flame to it for extra hit. The thing dodged at just the right moment as he scored a hard hit against Greensleeves. The arrow missed it, and Greensleeves dropped to the sand.

"Greensleeves!" Horc shouted and fired another arrow without focusing his shot or adding magic to it.

Just as Greensleeves' hands started to glow blue with a healing spell, the Hobgoblin stomped his mail boot hard on his head. Greensleeves' health bar in the group icons flashed red and went out.

Horc's arrow caught the Hobgoblin in the shoulder and didn't do much to drop its health.

"Damn it!" Horc fired again with an unfocused and un-augmented arrow. It caught the Hobgoblin in the side.

The enemy fighter laughed and pulled the arrow out. "You're going to have to do better than that, Ranger." It called as Wolf slammed into it.

It swung its axe hard, catching Wolf in the side, but it didn't slow him down much.

Horc took a deep breath and vowed to not repeat his mistakes as Greensleeves' corpse shimmered and vanished into pixels. "You really need to die," he muttered as he focused his shot and added Poison to it. The arrow streaked across the arena and hit the thing in the throat.

The Hobgoblin's health dropped to under half with the excellent blow. Then a pair of daggers went flying into it. Horc took a deep breath and fired another arrow with Flame on it. The daggers and the arrow hit in quick succession. The Hobgoblin caught fire and dropped to the sand to roll around, trying to put out the flames. It screamed as Wolf savaged its throat. Another round of knives and arrow finished it off.

Horc glanced at his display. Greensleeves' icon was there but had the same grayed-out effect as Steelmaiden and Slashers.

Greensleeves. Are you there? He frantically typed in group chat. His chest tightened. Something bad had happened when Greensleeves had died. They'd just lost their healer. Without Baladara, he and Tufkakes were going to be in a world of hurt trying to rescue everyone.

The iron gate covering the tunnel they'd come out of slowly rose.

Horc looked up to the high seats where Rothand had been, but the big Orc Halfling was gone.

"Not bad," Bo' called out as he scurried toward them. "Not great either. Yous lost yous' healer. Yous better hope yous' Mage comes back before yous' next bout. It would be bad if yous were down to just two of yous."

"What?" Horc started at the Goblin. "I thought we could only fight in groups of three or five."

Bo' shook his head. "Yous' group has to start with three or five, but if yous lose a member, yous have to keep fighting until yous either win, or are defeated."

Things sounded worse by the minute.

"So where is Greensleeves?" Horc demanded. "He's not dead anymore. I can see him on my screen."

"He's fighting for us now," Bo' replied, waving Horc and Tufkakes down the corridor. "It's in the contract yous guys agreed to when yous signed up to fight. If yous die in the arena yous become Rothand's property."

It was all Horc could do to not stumble. The AI was malfunctioning worse than they'd expected. There was something majorly wrong, and with their healer out of the picture, they were going to have to be more careful than ever. He needed to get word to Rick, maybe Rick could figure out something. Horc wondered if he'd be able to text Rick like he did his parents from the game. If they could get through to Rick, maybe he could pull Greensleeves out. Surely, he wouldn't want his husband stuck in the game. If they didn't do something soon, a lot of the players were going to be stuck in the game and how would Total Immersion Systems function if most of their employees were stuck in a game they were just supposed to be beta testing?

17

AS MUCH as he wanted to strangle Bo' Horc managed to keep it under control as they made it back to the 'best room in the place'.

"Yous guys get a couple hours to rest up and get yous health back up to full before the next bout," Bo' said. "If yous'd like something to eat, just let me know and I'll bring yous something."

"We'll let you know if we need anything," Tufkakes snapped.

"Fine, fine. If yous don't holler, I'll give you a half an hour warning." Bo' turned and hurried out of the room.

Tufkakes frowned at the door for a moment before turning to me. "I think we might want to worry about someone magically eaves dropping on us in here."

"And without magic users we won't be able to block it," Horc agreed, although he hadn't thought about anyone spying on them. When he did, it made a certain amount of sense. By spying on contestants, Rothand would have a better idea about what kinds of opponents to throw at them.

"Exactly." Tufkakes nodded. "What are we going to do?"

"See about getting Baladara back here for starters, then we need to figure out a way to let Rick know what happened to Greensleeves." Horc sat on the bed. "Let's hope Lisa's monitoring Mike's texts."

Since he'd linked his pod to his cell phone before he entered Halfworld, Horc pulled up the text interface. After a second, he found Mike's number.

Mike, or Lisa, we need help in game.

Horc wished he had David's number or some way to contact Rick to let him know what happened. He wasn't a great computer genius. He could provide customer support when they needed help with their pods, but that was more of an engineering and or marketing thing than a computer thing. Sure, sometimes he helped people figure out why their game wasn't connecting with the pods correctly, but for that he just looked things up, either in the minimal info the company provided, or through online searches of things other customers had figured out.

The online searches gave him an idea, he knew David's last name, maybe, with any luck, Rick had the same last name. Horc checked his game menu and pulled up the help screen. From going there early in his time on Halfworld, he knew there wasn't much in game, but there was the option to search the net outside the game systems. He only had to jump through a couple of technical hoops to get out of the game system and onto the World Wide Web. He did a search for Rick Remington first in the phone directory, then in various social media. Horc was surprised by how many Rick Remingtons there were. He narrowed his search down to Georgia.

Horc's text window beeped.

Alan, this is Lisa. Mike's still asleep. What's going on?

Horc breathed a sigh of relief as he turned his attention from the internet search to his text. At least something was working.

Lisa, we need Mike back in the game. We just lost Greensleeves in the first round of combat in the arena.

When he died, Rothand claimed him and we can't get him back in the party.

He paused and realized that was a fairly long text, then sent it anyway. It was easier than sending multiple texts.

Not good. Let me log in for him. We need to let him sleep.

You? Horc started to object, then remembered that Lisa was a gamer herself and helped Mike design his characters. Also, since Mike was still on VR helmet and gloves, she was probably watching most everything through a large screen monitor anyway.

I'm good with casters. Not great. Prefer sneaks.

Okay, sure. We need the firepower.

Good. Mike doesn't know it, but I gave him a little something to help him sleep.

Horc groaned, then realized Mike must've been a lot more tired than he was letting on. He knew Lisa, and she was very protective of Mike. If she slipped him something to help him sleep, it was probably because he'd been planning on getting back into the game as quickly as possible.

We've got a little while before they're going to come for our next round. No need to rush.

I'll log in shortly. Need to make sure the kids are covered since Mike's asleep and I'll be in game.

See you soon then.

Horc turned back to his internet search. There were only three Rick Remington's in Georgia. He asked Google maps to display the location of each one. All he knew was that David and Rick worked out of the Atlanta office, he wasn't sure where they lived, but figured Atlanta was like Dallas and most other large cities and had lots of suburbs where the people who worked in town might live. One of the Ricks lived in the far southwestern corner of Georgia so Horc didn't even bother with that one. He looked at the other two. They were both fairly close to downtown Atlanta, but on different sides of the city. To compare the two, he did a search for David Remington. That got him a hit that overlaid with the location or Rick Remington.

"Keep your fingers crossed, I might have him," Horc mumbled more to himself than to Tufkakes.

"Have who?" Tufkakes asked. "Oh, Greensleeves' husband."

"Hopefully." Horc put the number into his text app.

Rick, this is Horc. Ah, sorry, Alan Gosling. Trying to reach you about David.

Horc blinked and looked at Tufkakes. "Okay, send Rick a message, now to see if he gets it. If we don't get a response in a few minutes, I'll try some other social network stuff, or another number for a different Rick Remington. If it's not the right one, they either won't answer, or will reply something rude."

"In my neighborhood rude is more likely," Tufkakcs said. "I wonder if I should get you my info in case something stupid like this happens to me." Then he shook his head. "Nah, my kids won't be able to help out, even if they bothered to check their messages. Rick's more apt to be able to do something about the game."

"Right." Horc leaned against the wall and tried to ignore the straw bits sticking out of the mattress into his legs and butt.

His text notification beeped. He opened it and it filled his screen.

Horc, what happened? David's still online. His pod's working properly, but I can't reach him.

Rick. Glad I made the right choice. Nice something went easy for once in this game. Greensleeves died in our first bout in the arena and when he rezzed, Rothand claimed him as his. I can see him in party but can't reach him. Just like Steelmaiden and Slasher. Horc hated being the one telling Rick that his husband was in trouble, but he was the only option.

That's not good. Right now, the AI is sidestepping us every time we try to make an adjustment. We're going to have to take it all the way down to reprogram it, but we can't do that with you and the others stuck in there.

That didn't sound like good news. Horc frowned as he replied. *What can we do from here?*

I don't know. I'm going to look over David's game log, see if I can figure anything out from that, see the exact moment the AI took over. Maybe there's a clue there we can exploit.

Okay. A thought hit Horc as he sent the minimal message. *Did Rick tell you about the wall around the island and how it was appearing brick by brick?*

No, he didn't. That's good and bad. Good in that the AI hasn't figured out how to just make completed things appear. Bad because it's learned enough to understand how to make things by constructing the parts and putting them together. I'll relay this to the developer teams.

Hope it helps resolve this problem. Horc wasn't sure anything was going to be able to resolve the problem of the rogue AI.

System shows you and Tufkakes to still be in the arena. Part of me wants you to be safe, but I also want someone keeping an eye on David.

Our group motto is "Friends don't leave friends to die in dungeons" that applies to arenas too. I...ah...we'll stick by and make sure he can get out.

Right now, I'm only showing two of you. If you want, I can send more help.

Horc was tempted to ask him to find another group healer, but decided not to, just yet. *Baladara will be back online shortly. We can only have three players in the arena party at one time. If we lose another party member, I'll let you know.*

Okay. I'll make sure to keep my text app up and loud, so I don't miss anything.

Good. You're our god-like help, you and Miranda.

Thanks. Stay safe.

Horc sighed and then began to relay everything from Rick to Tufkakes. When he was done, he yawned. "Man, I'm tired now."

"No worries. I'll keep watch for you for a little while. Grab a quick nap and I'll wake you if anything goes wrong and I need to have your mighty bow." Tufkakes cracked his knuckles and settled on the bed across from Horc.

With Wolf at his side, Horc didn't bother trying to lie down on the lumpy, sticky mattress. He just closed his eyes and willed himself to sleep, leaning against the wall. Wolf whined and put his head in Horc's lap. Having his companion there with him was more relaxing and comforting than the bed itself.

A SOFT explosion brought Horc roughly out of his slumber.

"I don't understand how he can work these spells with them laid out like this," Baladara stood in the middle of the room with her hands out and a scowl on her face.

"Hi, Lisa," Horc said, stretching, the rubbing his eyes that felt like sandpaper. He could definitely use more than the little bit of sleep he'd gotten.

"Hi, Alan, or should I say Horc? I'm not as hardcore about gaming as Mike is." She got a faraway look for a moment. Then she blinked and nodded. "That should be better." She promptly started a spell, then broke the casting, her hands stopped glowing before it completed. "Definitely better."

"He's not going to be pissed that you played with his settings?" Tufkakes asked with a smirk from the bed across the Horc. It didn't look like he'd moved while Horc had been asleep.

"I do it all the time," Baladara turned in a tight circle. "Okay, I like this skirt, one of the better choices he could've made while I wasn't helping him with his clothing options, but I don't think this blouse does much for me." She ran her hands over the tight blue corset and white chemise. "Of course, I'm a little surprised he didn't go with a bikini again. But then, after we had a little discussion about that in a game a few months ago, he's been on good behavior with his wardrobe."

Tufkakes laughed. "Girl, it sounds like you keep him on a tight leash."

Baladara shrugged. "Not really. We like to play together from time to time. Right now, Halfworld isn't set up for spouses since it's still in beta. When it opens up, I'll be in here as much as Mike, if we can get folks to watch the kids. With VR, that's one of our rules, we can both play as long as we've got the kids covered. I had to wait for Mike's sister to get over and lend a hand this afternoon."

Horc sighed. He was so lost between the game and the real world he had no idea what time it was out there, or even what day it was. Everything was running together for him and it made him feel totally disconnected.

"Well, thanks for coming and filling in. With Greensleeves lost for the moment, we need a caster." Horc slipped off the bed and stretched again. His back hurt from sleeping sitting up, just like it would've IRL.

"Mike's given me a few hints about how real this place is." Baladara turned around as if studying their small room. "And I've been watching through the monitor but being here is so much more. When this game hits the shelves it's going to give Total Immersion Systems a major boost."

"If they can get the AI under control," Tufkakes said. "Nobody really wants to be running around in a game where you can get kidnapped by the AI and be unable to log out. Not cool."

"Yeah, there is that. I wonder if that's just for pod users, or if google and glove folks have to worry about that too." Baladara looked at her hands.

"Hey, we don't know for sure. Let's ask." Horc brought up his text window and fired off the question to Rick.

Just thought of something, are all the players being prevented from logging off pod users, or are some of them old school goggles and gloves?

His reply was almost instant. *Haven't looked at that angle yet. Will check and get back to you. Good question.*

"They don't know. They're going to look into it and let us know." A strange tingle ran down Horc's spine. He felt like someone was watching him. He turned and couldn't spot anything out of the ordinary in the room.

Just then the door opened and Bo' looked in. "This is yous thirty-minute warning. If yous need food or drink this is yous' last chance to ask for it." He paused and stared at Baladara. "Oh, your Elf Mage is back. Not that it's going to do yous much good."

"I think we're good on the refreshment side of things," Horc said. "Although I'll visit the little boys' room before we head out."

"I'll be back for yous in a few." Bo' turned and closed the door.

"Is Bo' short for Bowser?" Baladara asked. "Kinda an odd little guy."

Horc shrugged. "He's a Goblin, isn't that a bit repetitive?"

"Depends on the game." Baladara slapped her forehead. "Oh yeah, I forgot Mike said you're more of a science fiction player than a fantasy player."

"I've only done a few fantasy games," Horc said as he walked toward the door. The bathroom was a couple doors down. "Don't tell Mike, but this one is starting to grow on me. If I could log out it would be great."

"They've got your pod free of the house and are working on getting you out," Baladara said. "It's only a matter of time now."

"Yeah, and then we've got to get everyone else out too." Horc opened the door and headed out with Wolf at his heels. "I'll be right back."

Having Lisa filling in driving Baladara was a little odd, but it would give them the firepower they needed to stay alive, he just hoped she was a good enough player to pull it off. She hadn't started the toon from level one and brought her to the point she was. Although he knew of people buying high-level characters and never bothering to bring them up themselves, he always felt like players who ran a toon from the start had a better feel for what could be done in the game. He hoped Baladara would be able to pull her own weight in the arena and not end up like Greensleeves.

18

AGAIN BO' led them down the corridor to the arena sands.

"Remember, don't die," Tufkakes said as we walked. "None of us need to wind up like Greensleeves and the others."

Horc nodded but didn't say anything. He definitely didn't want to end up like the others had; somehow it made the idea of being trapped in the game that much scarier. The presence of Wolf at his side along with Tufkakes and Baladara at his back helped.

"The boss wants to see how yous guys handle a different type of crowd this time." Bo' stepped to the side and waved them into the arena.

Like before, the sands were empty. In the stands, there were a few more people than before. The big guy was back in his box seat. The others appeared to be players of different levels. They seemed to either be there to see how the arena worked, or just watch the spectacle that was about to unfold below them.

"This crowd?" Tufkakes pointed up at the seats encircling the arena.

Bo' chuckled and stepped back toward the spot where the gate would drop. "Nope, they're just lucky saps."

"Really charming," Baladara muttered under her breath.

Like before, the huge iron portcullis dropped once Bo' was past it.

"This whole place is charming." Horc pulled his bow and fitted an arrow, trying to be ready for whoever, or whatever came at them. His heart pounded like when he took an escalated phone call at work and the tech told him the customer was really pissed. There was no way of knowing if the person on the other end of the call would be remotely understanding, or just continue to rant. Waiting for whatever the arena masters were going to throw at them made his heart pound that same way, and he hated it just as much.

The gate on the opposite theirs rose and there was a lot of shouting, followed by roaring that sounded like an angry beast ready to tear someone's head off. It wasn't a sound Horc had ever heard before, but the tone of it reminded him of those angry customers and made him want to find a different line of work. But he couldn't log out, or even claim to be sick, he had to face whatever was coming his way.

The first thing to emerge from the tunnel lumbered out like a white bear on two legs, but there was something wrong with it. As it came into the light, it blinked, then tried to turn and go back into the tunnel. It cried out in pain. Its head was more cat-like than bear, but its ears were like a horse or deer. Long scratches marred its coat, exposing swatches of pink hide.

"Okay, that's weird," Baladara said. "I'm betting it's not natural."

"It's a game," Tufkakes said, bouncing her knives in her hand. "None of this natural, but it sounds scared, like it doesn't want to be here."

Horc shook his head. "Join the club. None of us want to be here."

Two big humanoids with spears thrust their weapons toward the beast. It whimpered and stepped farther out onto the sands.

Beside it came a huge gray thing on four legs that looked like a draft horse, with a bear's torso instead of a human's. It kicked out at the spearmen, but someone behind it cracked a whip. It reared up and screamed.

"Okay, so we're supposed to fight this magical menagerie?" Baladara asked. "They don't look like they're going to put up much of a fight. But I don't feel good about attacking them. They're kinda sad."

"I agree," Tufkakes said with a heavy frown. "This place gets more and more messed up."

Horc didn't like the idea of going after helpless animals, or hybrids, or whatever these things were. They were as much prisoners as Greensleeves and the others. They deserved to be freed, not fought.

"Why are there only two of them?" Horc asked as the spearmen and whipper turned and ran back to the corridor.

The gate clanged as it dropped into place.

"There's something else here," Baladara said. "Give me a second. I think I saw this spell on one of the other screens."

The two-legged foe pounded on the gate for a moment, as the centaur-like beast looked around like it had a little more intelligence. When it spotted the party, it nodded, then folded its knobby equine legs and lowered itself to the sands.

A chill went through Horc. It was like the thing understood what was happening, but knew they weren't exactly its enemy.

Boos and hisses rose from the seats around them. It sounded like the spectators were a little disappointed in the lack of instant combat.

A strange ripple of something invisible went through the arena. It was like a cool breeze on a hot afternoon.

"Got it." Baladara said, then her hands blurred in red as she cast Fireball. It didn't go off toward the two pitiful creatures who wanted nothing to do with the combat, but off toward something just to their left.

"Got what?" Tufkakes asked seconds before the Fireball hit something.

A humanoid appeared and rolled in the sand. He wore leathers reminiscent of the ones Greensleeves had worn when he'd been Human and not a Sand Elf.

The text over his head said **Salamando, Human, Beastmaster, Level 26**. He was another player who had either used an invisibility spell to be cloaked, or something else.

Salamando bowed toward them, then gestured at the two hybrids that strangely didn't have any text over them. Even when they'd faced familiars or seen other Rangers with companions, the bonded NPCs had had text over them identifying them as something. The Beastmaster's animals didn't have that. That alone was as strange as they were.

"Go for the player," Tufkakes said.

Horc liked the sound of that better than attacking the poor disoriented creatures he'd brought with him. But if the Beastmaster had power over them, like his class suggested, why had they been herded into the arena? There was something they were missing, but Horc liked the idea of having a foe he could attack and not worry about hurting. He focused his shot on Salamando and let an arrow fly at the same time Baladara launched another fireball.

The bear creature stumbled a step as it turned away from the gate, then it dropped to all fours and ran toward the Beastmaster. For a second it looked like it was going to attack him, but it threw itself between its master and their attack. The damage caused its health bar to flash, showing a drop of nearly a quarter of its health. It also revealed a name in white text, Cymeriabear.

That text was the first white text Horc had seen above players or monsters in the game. It added to the question of exactly what they were.

"Not cool." Baladara readied another spell.

"Leave him to me," Tufkakes said, then disappeared into the shadows.

Baladara send off a round of Magical Force Bolts. They zipped across the arena and seemed to be under more control than Fireballs were. The bolts of red energy zipped across the arena and dodged out of the way when the Cymeriabear moved to intercept them.

The other creature got to its feet and stood shaking in the sand. It was like it was fighting the Beastmaster for control. Sweat formed on its flanks. When Baladara's Bolts hit Salamando, the equine creature bared its teeth. With its bear face, it was impossible to tell if that was a sign of happiness, or anger.

The Beastmaster's health was down to a quarter, like the Cymeriabear. Horc didn't want to risk another arrow for fear of hitting the hapless creature.

"Wolf. Go for the Beastmaster." Horc pointed toward Salamando.

With a growl, Wolf followed his orders and bounded off. Horc pulled his sword and trailed after him.

Baladara got off another round of Magical Bolts. They skillfully avoided the Cymeriabear that tried to cut them off before it got in the way of Wolf going for Salamando.

As Horc closed in on the Beastmaster, the equine creature jolted to its feet and reared up. It snarled and shook its head as it turned toward Salamando. Again, it stopped and stood shaking, the sweat from its flanks fell to the sand. Moisture beaded Salamando's forehead, and Horc was sure the Beastmaster battled his beast for superiority.

Tufkakes appeared behind Salamando and plunged a dagger into his back just as Wolf leapt up and clamped down on his crotch. The Beastmaster screamed in pain. His health flashed to under a quarter, blinking red.

The interruption in his concentration was the opening the controlled beasts needed. They spun and went for the Beastmaster. Horc took his opening and swung his sword. It hit the Beastmaster in the neck at the same time the Cymerabear tore his chest out.

Salamando dropped to the sand, lifeless.

Horc's XP bar flashed.

Level 23

Tufkakes and Baladara also leveled.

The two controlled bests faded away.

The crowd booed again.

Horc glanced up at the box where Rothand had been. Again, the pirate lord left, presumably as soon as the winner was obvious. It reminded him so much of upper management at work, they never stuck around for things, but had more important things to do than congratulate employees, or in this case, the entertainment, for jobs well done.

BY THE time they got back to their rooms, although Horc was starting to think of the place as their cell, his message indicator was flashing in his peripheral vision.

"Let me see who this is." Horc sat on the closest bed and opened the message window.

The message was from Rick.

Hey, monitoring you and the people you're engaging with. Thought it might be helpful in figuring out what's going on.

What have you learned? Horc eased back against the wall.

Something odd happened when the Beastmaster died. I'm not really sure what it was. He respawned quickly, in the graveyard and was escorted back to the cells under the arena. But there was like a split second where everything read normal.

A jolt of possibility went through Horc. *Do you think he could've logged out, if he'd been ready for it?*

I don't know.

What about his creatures having white text. Is that normal? Horc knew there was a lot about Halfworld he didn't know, but even things like that were supposed to have rules.

The beasts that a Beastmaster controls are conjured, sort of like the demons a Warlock or the undead a Necromancer calls. They are more products of the Beastmaster's imagination, but they have a will of their own, like any animal. It's the most convoluted class we built into the game. There aren't that many people playing it yet, but the things they're coming up with are straight out of nightmares in some cases. We're thinking about taking out the part of making their creatures things from their own imagination, since we'd intended the conjured creatures to be things out of the real world. Beta testing.

Okay, but why did they have to be herded into the arena? That's weird.

It took a couple of seconds for Rick's answer to start appearing in their chat window. *He probably summoned them a while ago and then didn't try to control them until he needed to. It was a smart move to save mana. It would've allowed him to be more creative in their creating. If he was going for calling something quickly, he'd have probably had to just summon a dog, or wolf, or tiger, or something like that. Taking time in the casting lets him be more creative. It's something new we've worked into Halfworld and it only works on pod players. With the glove and goggle group they can just summon from a set list.*

It might be a little less creepy if they stuck to things off a list. Horc replied. He was supposed to be providing beta tester feedback and this was a good opportunity to do that.

I'll discuss that with the other designers once we get everyone out and the AI down. Strange class issues aren't nearly as important at this point as getting you guys to safety.

Right. I guess now we wait for our next call to battle.

Yes. I'll be monitoring that too. Maybe I can see something that will confirm we have a chance to get folks out. I really hope David is doing okay.

I was thinking about sending Tufkakes on a scouting mission again. Maybe he can find out something. Although Horc hated the idea of splitting up the party again. But if Tufkakes was fast, they might get the valuable info they needed.

That would be awesome. Ask him to tell David I'm trying really hard to get him out.

I will. Even though it was just words on the screen, Horc thought he could feel the emotion Rick put behind them and wondered what it would be like to have someone outside the game, other than his mother and father, pulling for him to get out and resume his normal life.

Rick signed off, and Horc sat there for a few minutes thinking about things. He hated the way his mind kept drifting to his real life and how much of the world he was missing. He wanted more and kept hoping he'd find a way to make it happen. He was going to get out of Halfworld and figure out what he really wanted to do with his life. He just had to.

19

TUFFCAKES CAME back in less than an hour, waking Horc from the short nap he was getting in between bouts.

"Man, I think the AI, or the pirates…one is upping their game in grabbing players." Tufkakes appeared in the middle of their room after the door opened and closed seemingly of its own volition.

"Are there more players in the cells?" Baladara asked, rising from the cross-legged pose she'd been sitting in for a while.

Horc had been noticing little things like the cross-legged pose that were tells, to him at least, that someone other than Mike was driving the toon. Their language was similar enough with Lisa only having a few outbursts that weren't things Mike would say, but they'd apparently been married long enough they sounded fairly alike.

"Yeah. The cells down there are nearly packed full. They've got Greensleeves in a different cell from Steelmaiden and Slasher. I passed on the info. Greensleeves is doing his best to stay in good humor during all this crap going on. I don't know Steelmaiden, but she sounds like she's about to start ripping people's heads off."

Letting out a long breath, Horc nodded. "That's Steelmaiden alright."

"Good." Tufkakes walked over to their small table and poured a glass of water from the steel carafe Bo' had brought and refilled while they were in the arena. It was nice to have the water available when they returned from a fight. "Now we need to get ready for the next round.

They might be getting a lot of players under their control, but I don't think we're getting a ton of players coming to the arena of their own free will."

"So, you're saying there's a lot of them and not a lot of us." Baladara sat on the bed and smoothed her skirts, another non-Mike action.

"Yeah, but there does seem to be more free players coming in." Tufkakes returned the metal cup to the table next to the carafe.

"But they only stay free until they die in their first battle and then they're Rothand's prisoners." Horc ran a hand through his rumpled black hair. "Okay. We need to work faster here. Still haven't heard back from Rick on any of his ideas-"

The door creaked open, interrupting his thoughts. Bo' stood there with a sheepish look on his green face. "Hey yous guys. I know it wasn't a long rest, but we're nearing the end of the day and the boss was wondering if yous'd be up for another bout this evening…say in about half an hour."

Horc glanced at the other two. The short nap and the water had helped him out a lot. His health bar and mana were back up to full. Both Tufkakes and Baladara nodded. "Sure. We can do it."

Bo' grinned. "Awesome. Thanks. I'll let the boss know yous guys are up for it. Thanks." He closed the door and shuffled off.

"I wonder if we shouldn't get Rick to put out a system warning telling players to avoid the arena," Tufkakes asked, taking a seat on the bed next to Horc's.

"I doubt the AI would let a system warning like that get out," Baladara said. "Aren't they supposed to be smarter than that?"

Horc nodded. "Yeah, I would think so anyway. This one is learning quickly. But if he put it out as a corporate message that went through email, that might either alert people before they entered the game, or if they have their email and other messaging tied to their pods, warn them that way."

"At this point they should shut down the beta program until they've made some fixes," Tufkakes muttered. "Maybe they have an uncorrupted backup of the AI they can upload once everyone's logged out and can get it running again soon."

"Not a bad idea." Horc brought up his message app and sent Rick their suggestions. It didn't take long to get a reply.

I like the ideas. I'll bounce them past upper management to get permission. Folks up there are getting touchy about things. Any idea when you're going back into the arena?

Half an hour. Horc replied. *No idea what we're fighting this time.*

I can work with that. I'll send the message up, then keep an eye on your party and see what I can see.

It made Horc feel better that Rick was watching out for them. Sure, it wasn't a for-sure way to stay alive, but then there would at least be a record of what happened if something went wrong. Horc wrapped up their conversation, then looked at Baladara and Tufkakes. "Okay. Rick's going to watch and see what he can learn."

"We need to try to kill them fast, so they don't hurt us, and to give him the data he needs." Tufkakes flexed her fingers, making her claws come out in a cat-like fashion.

"Sounds like a plan," Baladara said.

Horc wasn't sure about a plan that involved killing as many players as they could, but it did make sense. It was in the name of science after-all, and they would be able to respawn after a few minutes. Still he kept going back to the pain he felt during battle and wondered if there was pain associated with dying in Halfworld. He didn't know for sure and didn't like the idea of hurting other people. But the AI was hurting them, and unless he could do something to stop it, the machine intelligence would continue to hurt them.

AGAIN, HORC'S heart raced as the portcullis closed behind Bo'. He hated the feeling and tried to push it down as he stood in between Baladara and Tufkakes with Wolf slightly in front of them.

Across from them, the gate slowly rose, and a voice boomed out.

"And the challengers, the Righteous Band!" It sounded like it came from everywhere and nowhere at the same time.

"That's new," Baladara said, flexing her hands. "I wonder if they do that for us and we're so far down the tunnel we can't hear it."

"We don't have a group name," Tufkakes muttered. "If we did they'd announce us when we come in, or at least that's what Bo' said on the first fight."

Horc shrugged and pulled an arrow. "I don't care one way or the other. We're in this to sort out saving our friends."

The Righteous Band entered the arena. It was three Paladins. They were higher level than the last time Horc had seen them, and he wasn't surprised they were there, Tufkakes and Baladara had told him Stan and the other mailroom guys were also in cells under the arena, right next to Steelmaiden and Slasher.

"Oh geez, not you guys," Stanishollyshmite said as the three of them stopped a short distance away.

"Yeah, us," Tufkakes shouted back, then dropped his voice. "These are the guys from the cell next to Steelmaiden. Baladara said something about them being total pricks. Not to mention that the lead guy can't spell."

"That's one way to look at them in game," Horc said, his voice equally low. "IRL, they're just looking for an easy path through life."

"We need to take them out, strictly for research," Baladara said with a wicked glint in her eyes.

"For research." Tufkakes laughed and disappeared into the shadows.

"Where'd he go?" Lefthandofgod asked, looking around frantically.

"He's a Rogue, fool," Righthandofgod snapped, punching Left's shoulder before pulling out his sword.

"He can just disappear? That doesn't seem right." Left looked confused.

Knowing how many inner-office memos the guys managed to lose for hours to days, Horc knew they weren't the sharpest tacks in the box. It wasn't that hard to keep track of the memos, especially since most inner-office communications were done via email and management was talking about doing away with inn-office memos completely.

"Not godly, at least," Stanishollyshmite agreed, then looked at Horc and Baladara. "You guys know this isn't anything personal."

"And you remember none of us are supposed to do anything that puts Horc in danger, don't you?" Baladara's tone as sharp and no-nonsense.

"I thought the rules had changed here in the arena," Stanishollyshmite argued swinging his sword around with more agility than he should've been able to have considering the thing was almost as wide as he was and looked completely unwieldy.

"Not in any memo we've gotten," Horc replied. As he unleashed his arrow, he reminded himself that the mailroom guys would come back if they died, they still weren't sure if he would be so lucky.

The arrow somehow sailed through Stanishollyshmite's attempt to block with his massive sword and caught the Paladin in the throat. Stanishollyshmite dropped his sword and grabbed his neck. "Get it out." He gurgled. As the critical shot appeared in Horc's vision and Stanishollyshmite's health dropped to half.

"Gladly." Tufkakes appeared out of the shadows and rammed his dagger into the base of the Paladin's skull.

As Stanishollyshmite's health dropped into the red and started flashing. Tufkakes reached around and twisted the arrow, ramming in deeper into the Paladin's throat. Stanishollyshmite dropped to the sand as his health bar blinked one last time and faded away.

"Get off him!" Righthandofgod shouted and rushed Tufkakes with a sword that was nearly as big as Stanishollyshmite's had been.

"Same to you." Baladara got off a fireball knocking Right back a couple of feet.

Horc sent his next arrow at Lefthandofgod. Wolf followed the arrow, turning from where he'd been running toward the last target, the downed Stanishollyshmite.

Somehow, Left managed to bat the arrow away, sending it clattering into the wall to his right. Horc added Poison to the next arrow and focused his shot. Left came running and was almost too close when Horc loosed his shot. It caught Left in the face, barely missing his eye.

Wolf slammed into Left as the Paladin screamed and tore at the arrow sticking out of his cheek. He managed to keep hold of his sword with one hand, but the tip of the massive blade rested uselessly on the arena sand.

Horc dropped his bow and pulled his sword. He might've been able to back up a few feet and get off more shots while Left yanked the arrow out of his check, but he didn't bother. From the little he'd seen of the guy's fighting skills they were about as good at gaming as they were at keeping the mailroom running. Even if he managed to land a few good hits with that ridiculous sword of his, it wouldn't be enough to kill Horc.

With Wolf tearing at the back of Left's neck, Horc swung at his sword arm, hoping to disarm him.

Left finally pulled the arrow out and managed to get his sword up in time to block. "Dude, not cool attacking while I was distracted. It ain't right."

Horc stepped back and blocked Left's swing. "All's fair in love and war."

"Rumor has it you don't know about love." Left swung again.

Ducking under the blow, Horc slashed up with his sword. "And you do? Dude, I've watched you drooling over Melinna in accounting. Pathetic." Since they were in the game, he really hoped nothing he said came back to haunt him. He scored a good hit and with the damage from the arrow and Wolf's attack, he'd dropped Left to less than three quarters. The Poison from the arrow would continue to drain him for another two rounds of battle.

"Melinna is pretty, not that you'd have noticed." Left kicked at Horc as Horc dropped and rolled away, trying to put a little distance between them.

"I know Melinna is pretty, I just don't spend time drooling over something I can't have." Horc came up in a crouch and waited for Left to reach him. That big sword was a definite disadvantage no matter how impressive it must look to the Paladin.

"Everyone knows you don't care about anyone at work." Left hefted the sword high and started to bring it down on Horc. "It's just weird."

"No, Dude, it's not weird." Horc dove out of the way and again came up inside Left's guard and slashed him hard across the right arm. He was down to half health. "It's called not dating in the work place. That's not cool." He wasn't bothered by the fight talk, and it was helping keep Left distracted.

"We're supposed to be finding ourselves women so we can have children and keep the house of God going strong." Left let go of his sword and punched Horc in the face. The damage flashed red on his screen but didn't even knock him down by a noticeable amount.

"Our world is over populated in case you failed to notice." Horc swung hard at the same spot on Left's right arm he'd hit before. Blood sprayed his face.

Left stumbled away from him, down to nearly a quarter. "Damn it. That hurts."

"This game does that." Horc pressed his attack, swinging his sword, slicing for Left's head. "Come on, Dude, give up."

"No." Left managed to get his sword up to block part of the blow, but Horc scored at nearly the same spot on Left's cheek as he had with his arrow.

Left's health flashed orange.

"Oh, for heaven's sake." Baladara's Fireball caught Left in the side of the ear. His head exploded as his health bar went red and then disappeared altogether.

Around the stadium the crowd whose noise had disappeared as Horc concentrated on defeating Left, roared its approval of their victory. The sound of the cheers made Horc's heart race and he got light-headed. He wasn't used to hearing admiration from fans. The most he normally got was a good report on a monitored phone call.

Horc wiped the bodily fluids off even as they began to pixelate and disappear. "I think you overdid that one."

"Maybe, but these guys are a bigger pain than even they realized." Baladara shook out her hands like they were cramping.

"Yeah, they were," Tufkakes agreed, limping toward Horc. "Those damned swords don't need to be all that agile, all they have to do is land a good hit and they can do some major damage."

"You okay?" Horc went to lend Tufkakes a shoulder.

"Sure. Nothing a bit of food and time off my feet won't cure." Tufkakes health bar was under a half. It was the worst Horc had seen since Greensleeves had died and been captured.

Out of reflex, Horc glanced up at Rothand's box. Their large tormentor had only just turned away to leave. It was the longest he'd stayed to watch a fight. Horc wondered if there was some significance to that or not.

With a shrug, he turned toward the rising gate where Bo' stood waiting for them. He hoped Rick got some useful information from the decimation of the Righteous Band. It felt weird to make-believe kill co-workers, but it was also somewhat cathartic. Since the others didn't work with the guys, he doubted they'd feel the same, but he figured if Mike had been driving Baladara, they'd have high-fived after Lefthandofgod's head exploded.

20

HORC STARED at Rick's message.

We're still analyzing the data we got to try to figure out what it means, but there's definitely a split second at the time of resurrection that everything on the account is normal.

If someone is ready when they die, they might be able to log out? Horc hoped that was right. Not that it helped him, but it would help the others trapped in the game.

I don't know if they'd be able to do it by themselves. But I might be able to pull them out, or one of my team. We're going to set up someone to try next time the arena starts up again.

Bo' said we'd get the night off, which is good. Tufkakes was hurt pretty bad, but he'll recover. Horc hated the idea that another of his team might end up in Rothand's menagerie.

That'll give us more time to work, and maybe time to sleep. Game time is a little faster than our time. It helps keep the global game from bogging down for anyone that way.

Don't kill yourself with this. We need your brain at its peak functioning just like we need us working at top performance. That's the only way we're all getting out of this.

Right. Miranda wanted me to tell you she's got a hardware team trying to diagnose your pod's problems, but there's a bug there too.

Horc chuckled as he replied. *No kidding.*

"Is Rick being funny?" Baladara asked.

"Not exactly." Horc muttered as Rick ended their connection and he stretched. At least they were going to get a little down time.

"WHAT IN the bloody hell did that woman do to my controls?" Baladara's shouts woke Horc.

He yawned and stretched feeling like it had just been a few minutes since he'd stretched the last time. His neck was sore from sleeping against the wall, but he was still fairly sure it was probably more comfortable that way than laying down on the straw mattress.

"Sounds like Mike's back in the driver's seat," Tufkakes said before yawning himself.

"How long were we out?" Horc asked, easing off the bed so he could bend and get his back to pop.

"Long enough," Baladara replied. "Did neither one of you care enough to keep her from playing with my tool bars? I mean geez, she's got everything laid out by casting time, longest to shortest. How's a guy supposed to get his spells off like this. I hate it when she plays with my hotkeys. " Her hands were flailing around like crazy.

"It wasn't our idea to let Lisa slip you a mickey and then take over. Hope you're up to a few more rounds in the arena." Tufkakes walked over to the table with the container of water. There were some fruit and rolls on it next to the water. "Looks like Bo' or someone came in here while we were out and left us breakfast."

"At least something around here is working," Baladara muttered and suddenly stopped gesturing. "Okay. I think I've got everything back to normal. Geez. I don't think I'm ever letting her drive my toons again, or at least not while I'm not in the room watching her do it."

Horc picked up a piece of fruit, still surprised at how real it felt in his hands. It was red like a pomegranate and when he pulled out his knife and cut into it, the flesh inside smelled like he expected. As he started scraping out the seeds and flesh, the door opened and Bo' walked in. Horc really wished the Goblin understood basic courtesies like knocking.

"Ah, again yous are up and ready to fight." Bo' beamed in obvious delight. "This is good. The boss was very impressed with yous defeat of the Paladins last night. He's asking for insulting of yous foes today. The way Horc verbally laid into Lefthandofgod made the boss laugh, and the spectators too."

"Let's just say we don't always see eye to eye at work," Horc said as a bit of fruit juice ran down his jaw.

Bo' laughed. "I totally get yous there."

Tufkakes yawned again. "So how long do we have this time?"

"Thirty minutes like always. Is there anything else yous all need before the fight?" Bo' seemed to study each of them for a moment. "Looks like yous all recovered for the last battle."

Horc did a quick look at the party stats, everyone, even the ones grayed out, were good on health and mana. "I think we're good." He took another bite of his fruit.

"Good, good." Bo's turned back to the door. "See yous guys soon."

Horc finished his fruit and returned to the spot on the bed he was beginning to think of as his and rubbed Wolf between the ears. For good measure, he opened his bag and pulled Wolf out a chunk of meat. "You're doing good, Boy." Then Horc sighed. "Okay. Let me check with Rick and see if he's got anything for us. If we're going to be fighting soon he needs to know."

"Definitely. I hope I get some good data for that epic fight I missed out on." Baladara went for a piece of fruit too. "I'm not going to tell them, but I was hoping for a chance to kick those mailroom guys while we were in here, and what happened? I missed it."

"It was fairly gratifying." Grinning at the memory, Horc opened up the chat window and sent Rick an inquiry.

Hey Alan, you about ready to get the day going?

I guess. What did you programmers find out on your end?

Good news. Looks like that window might be what we've been looking for. Drawback is right now I've only got me and one other tech standing by to grab people as they resurrect.

Horc sighed and rested his head against the wall. *So, we're not going to be able to even get a team of three out at a time.*

Depends. If you do it the way you did last night with the bible boys, you could. Kill one off fast and draw the other two out. That would give us time to yank the first one as they rez and then be ready for the others a couple of minutes later.

If we do it close together then, it's bad. Horc was hoping for something a little easier than trying to time the deaths, and time the rez grabs. That was an awful lot of timing for pulling people out of a game.

Not exactly bad, we'll still be able to get them out, just not that time. You'll need to kill them again.

An idea hit Horc. *Okay, question. Are you only going to be able to catch people who die close to us, or will you be able to catch anyone who dies in the arena?*

There was a pause in the response.

Right now, we're having a bit of difficulty trying to get a wide view of what's going on in the game. We can watch you and the people you're interacting with because it's a focused view. Trying to keep track of everyone in the arena would be a no go at this moment.

Then you're saying we're going to have to be a good enough team to take down everything they throw at us? A sense of dread settled into Horc's stomach. That means our own people.

We're working on getting a wide view of what's going on.

The door opened and Bo' came in. "Okay yous guys. It's time to fight again."

Gotta go. It's show time.

Not waiting for Rick's response, Horc hopped off the bed and walked with his friends out of the room and down the corridor toward the arena and the start of the contest for the day. If they were going to have to take out all the captive players, he hoped it was going to be a good day and not one that sucked big time. Although he felt like he was walking into a meeting with upper management with mustard on a red tie and grease stains on his shirt and not wanting to ask what more could go wrong.

21

WHEN THE gate across the arena opened, Horc's heart nearly stopped. Steelmaiden stood there looking grim. Her armor was dented and scuffed worse than he'd ever seen it. She was always right on top of keeping her armor and weapons repaired and ready for battle. The woman standing across from him wasn't the same woman who was part of their party, she was something rougher, meaner, almost desperate. Her appearance was so bad, Horc only caught a glance of the number of people filling that stands. It seemed like nearly every concrete seat was filled.

"This doesn't look good," Baladara said grimly.

"I've never seen her, except through the bars of a cell, but she looks like hell," Tufkakes added.

Horc nodded. "That she does. First goal, somebody get close enough to her to let her know about our plan. She needs to be ready to attempt to log out when she rezs." He wasn't sure he could be the one to take her down. The idea of hurting a friend, even for their own good, didn't sit well with him.

"That might not be so easy." Baladara pointed to the two huge bears flanking the Barbarian woman.

"Yeah, that looks even nastier." Horc tried to study the bears and determine what they were and how powerful, but there was nothing above their heads. "Looks like they might've gotten another Beastmaster."

"Or the same one," Tufkakes said. "I'll find him and take him out. Hold off on Steelmaiden until he's down.

It'll be easier that way." He stepped back into the shadows of the wall and disappeared from view.

"Sounds good." Horc notched an arrow. The ones Tufkakes had found were diminishing to short supply. He was going to have to make every one count.

Focusing on the largest bear, Horc let a Fire arrow fly as the distant gate fell with a clang. Since the bears didn't have to be herded into the arena like the cymeras had been, he presumed they were easier for the Beastmaster to control, or they faced a different foe, one who was more powerful than the previous one.

The bear roared as Horc's arrow caught it in the eye and set its fur on fire.

Horc quickly readied another arrow and let it fly as Wolf hit the same bear he'd injured.

Baladara's first Fireball hit the other bear, knocking it over backward as it surged onto its hind legs. That bear also caught on fire, but it got back to its feet quickly. The flaming bear then roared and charged the Elven Mage.

Horc managed to get off two more arrows before the bear closed on him. Wolf was doing his best to distract the bear, but it seemed to be useless as it focused its efforts on getting to Horc. Without a health bar, it was impossible for Horc to tell how much damage he was doing, other than the numbers scrolling past his vision indicating that his efforts were having effects. He wished he could see more and know how close to down the bear was as he drew his sword and set his feet in preparation for the thing to hit him.

The charging bear hit him hard, forcing him back a couple of feet and taking a chunk out of his health points.

Horc swung his sword as hard as he could.

A critical hit notification flashed on his screen showing a hundred points in damage. Then the beast stumbled.

Taking advantage of its obvious weakness, Horc cleaved it again. Another critical hit scrolled past. The bear dropped to the sand and pixelated. The crowd in the seats above him cheered.

"I don't want to do this." Steelmaiden hit him hard in the face with the pommel of her sword.

Horc stumbled backward, trying to get his sword up as his head spun with the blow. He was down under three quarter's health.

"Then don't." Horc circled away from her as Wolf hit her from behind.

Steelmaiden reached back for Wolf, but he was already gone, doing his best to stay out of reach.

Horc took the distraction, lowered his shoulder toward her chest and charged. He hit her hard, carrying her down and landing hard enough on the sand to send up a plume of dust.

"Log out when you rez," he said softly, hoping she heard him.

She hit him hard in the shoulder, again with her pommel.

Rolling away, Horc staggered to his feet. His shoulder felt numb, and he was thankful it hadn't been his sword arm.

Rushing him, she brought her sword down in a vicious cut that he only barely blocked. Their blades rang out and she leaned in close to him. "Won't help. No time to log out." She shoved away from him.

Wolf dashed behind her and Horc shoved her back over the companion just as a Fireball shot across the arena.

Steelmaiden fell hard, just as Wolf scooted past her with the barest yelp when she landed on the tip of his tail.

Horc frowned as he pounced on her. "Be ready. You have to log out as you rez. Rick's standing by to grab you and get you out."

His gloved hand throbbed from impacting the steel of her helmet.

"Worth a try." Steelmaiden shoved Horc away. "Give me your best shot."

"Horc, look out!" Baladara shouted.

Some instinct made him drop to the sands and roll. A heavy thunk sounded above him as Horc came to his knees.

In the list of party avatars, Steelmaiden's began to flash bright red.

Wolf hit her hard, knocking her back into the sands.

Horc glanced at his own health bar as hers went out. His was down to a quarter.

Steelmaiden shimmered, then pixelated out of existence.

A dagger flashed toward Horc as he dodged out of the blade's way. He looked in the direction the dagger had come from. Seconds later, Tufkakes and a scrawny man in black leather armor rolled out onto the sands looking like they'd just fallen from the wall that encircled the arena.

"That's got to be the Beastmaster," Baladara moved a little to the right, as if to get a clearer shot as Tufkakes drove another dagger into the player and got a drop in his opponent's health for his efforts.

After the bears, whose health he couldn't see, it was nice to watch a health bar drop as Horc fired an arrow and caught the man in the side of the head. Another critical hit flashed on the screen as the Beastmaster's health dropped to under a quarter and turned orange.

Baladara's Fireball also caught it in the side of the head. There was a flash and gray matter splashed out on Tufkakes.

"Warn a guy about that next time." Tufkakes swiped at the gook even as it digitized and vanished.

"Sorry. Didn't realize he was that low." Baladara shook out her hands as the crowd roared its approval and stood.

The cheers went on for a solid minute. Horc had never had so many people ecstatic about something he'd done. Even though he wanted to get back to the cell so he could eat and drink to bring his health and mana back up, there was something about the admiration of strangers that made him want to stand there for a while and just soak it in.

As the gate they entered through came up, the spell of the crowd died down.

With a heavy sigh, Horc turned to where Bo' the Goblin was waiting for them to clear the arena so the next match could begin.

"Wonder why they didn't send both Slasher and Steelmaiden after us?" Baladara muttered as they headed for the gate.

"No clue," Horc replied. "I just hope she managed to get out. If we have a way to help people, we'll have to spread the word." It would make him feel better if at least someone was making progress in escaping the game.

WHEN THEY reached their cell, a large tray of food and drink was waiting for them. It was full of various fruits, breads and meats. The smell of the warm breads and roasted meat made Horc's mouth water.

"The boss is pleased with yous performance, even against yous former friend," Bo' gestured to the tray. "Enjoy his gratitude. I'll be back for yous all in a couple of hours."

Although the constant fighting was getting tiring, Horc nodded. "We'll be ready."

Bo' walked toward the door. "Good. The players are coming from near and far to watch yous guys." Horc waited from him to close the door before turning to the platter of food.

Tufkakes tossed a couple of slices of ham to Wolf. "You did a good job out there, Boy."

"We all did." Baladara grabbed something that looked like a yellow peach.

"I'm going to check with Rick." Horc really wanted to grab something to eat but finding out if Steelmaiden was safe was his top priority.

Sitting on the bed, he knew he didn't have to be seated in order to access his text app, but he didn't like texting while driving or walking, Horc brought up his texting app and sent Rick a message.

How'd it go?

Rick's response was almost instant, like he'd been sitting with his own text app open, waiting for Horc's message.

We got them both. Mariann…Steelmaiden, will be back with you shortly. We're getting her new toon ready to roll.

Horc frowned. *New toon?*

Steelmaiden is known to the AI. She's even changing pods as we speak. A friend of hers who lives near her is letting her borrow a pod for this.

After what she'd been through, Horc was a little surprised she'd be coming back online so soon. *She doesn't need to do that. We can get out without putting her at risk again.*

She's a feisty one. She wanted to go right back in, but I talked her into waiting for me to design her a new character, just to be safe.

Horc chuckled. Feisty was one way to describe Steelmaiden, and he wasn't surprised she was similar IRL. *You'll give us a warning as to who and what she is?*

You bet. We want her as part of your party. We should be ready to go before the next round.

That might take some convincing Bo' it'll be okay. Horc remembered how the Goblin had objected to them having four people when they'd first entered the arena and decided to be part of the games.

When that happens, I'll have to see what I can do to make things smoother. No worries. We'll work something out. It'll also give us an idea of what the AI is thinking.

Sounds like a plan. I'm going to go get something to eat now and rest a bit before the next round.

You do that. Try to avoid the close hand to hand next time. Your health dropped a little too low for comfort.

Will do my best. Horc closed the app and looked over at Tufkakes, Baladara and Wolf eating in silence.

"Did they get them both?" Tufkakes asked, pointing his banana at Horc. "As I Backstabbed the Beastmaster, I whispered to him to log out as he rezzed."

Horc nodded. "He said they had them both. Steelmaiden will be back with us shortly. They're getting her a new toon." Horc pursed his lips and glanced around the cell. "I wonder how we would tell if the AI is listening."

Baladara shook her head. "No clue. That does kinda add a new angle to this whole thing, doesn't it?"

"It does, and not one I like." Horc slid off the bed and walked over to pick up a large roll that after tearing it opened, he stuffed meats and cheeses into.

"You know, I really don't want to spend every minute in this damned cell worrying about what we're talking about." Baladara chewed her banana.

"Guess you don't have any cone of silence spells, or anything like that?" Tufkakes asked.

Baladara frowned. "And then what, we write everything down, or use sign language?" She shook her head. "Won't do us any good. I guess that's going to be our biggest hurdle in this adventure, out smarting an AI whose program we exist in at the moment."

A chill went through Horc. He didn't like the idea they wouldn't be able to plan things out. But the others were right, if the AI had figured out how to listen in on them, they might be in a world of hurt when it started using their plans against them.

22

A SLIGHT shimmer in the middle of the room announced Steelmaiden's arrival, although the green text over her head read **Titanya, Human, Warrior, Level 25**. Her armor was dark chain mail from head to toe, and her sword was a massive two-handed beast that looked like it could kill its opponents by weight alone.

"Hi Guys, miss me?" She grinned as she looked around the room.

Baladara whistled. "Damn, Girlfriend, you look more dangerous than ever."

Titanya frowned at her. "Please, don't girlfriend me. You're a married straight man playing a female character. I'm really picky about who calls me girlfriend, and at this point, you don't fit the bill. Besides what would your wife say?"

Baladara laughed. "And how do you know I'm not Lisa?"

"She's got a point," Horc added, stifling his own laugh. "Lisa was driving the toon for a bit while Mike got some sleep. If you know the two of them, you can spot the differences in them. I know this is Mike."

"What differences?" Baladara put her hands on her hips and objected. "This is a game. How can you tell one driver from another?"

Just the look of indignation on his face made Horc laugh. "One of these days I'll let you know."

"You guys got a nicer flat than we had below." Titanya gave the place another look. "At least you don't look as much like prisoners as Slasher and Greensleeves do at the moment."

"But we have an out," Tufkakes said. "Tell you what, why don't I see about slipping through the shadows and letting folks down below know that we have a plan."

Horc nodded. "Yeah, Bo' will probably be showing up soon for our next round of combat, so if you slip out now, Steelmaiden…I mean Titanya can be our third."

"I can handle these fools," Titanya said. "What I want is a shot at the pirate lord, Rothand. He's got things to answer for."

"It's the AI," Horc corrected, "but we've got to get everyone out of the game so we can bring it down, and before we can do that, we've got to get all the prisoners free."

"And someone needs to tell all those fool players in the stands their lives are in danger if they sign up to fight in the arena." Titanya started to sit on the bed nearest the door, then stopped half way down. She bounced the bed slightly and frowned. "Yeah, still better than down below, but no." She straightened and went to lean against the doorframe.

"We haven't gotten fleas or bedbugs yet." Horc said and then wondered if the game had been programmed to have such minute details.

"Be thankful." Titanya frowned and shook her head. "Both are all over the place downstairs. I wasn't sure what it was going to take to get rid of them from Steelmaiden. Not playing that toon again until someone tells me what to do there. The damn bugs itch like crazy."

"You know, you make me thankful I'm not in a pod," Baladara said with a sly grin.

"We can fix that," Titanya said.

"Anyway," Horc said. "Rick says they're trying to convince players to not come to the island and get wrapped up in the arena, but most of them aren't listening. It's like they don't care if they get caught up in the arena and can't log out."

"We work with these people," Baladara said. "We know how they can be at work, games only make them that much worse."

"She has a point," Titanya agreed. "I know the stands had more players in them each time I entered the arena."

"Agreed." Horc leaned against the wall, trying to think of some way to get the other players to log out and wait for the fix to stop the AI before things got worse. But the others were right. Nobody had ever heard of someone getting stuck in a game. They probably thought it was some kind of hype to get more people playing in an attempt to figure out what's going on.

"While you guys discuss this, I'm hitting the shadows." Without another word, Tufkakes faded away.

"Well, he's interesting," Titanya said. "Nice addition to the party."

"That's one way to look at him," Baladara said. "The stuffed animal look takes some getting used to."

Titanya shook her head. "I don't think so. I considered doing either a Procyan or an Ursan, but Human Fighter still gets better buffs. I was surprised the Ursans get Druid buffs, but not Barbarian or Fighter buffs. Procyans just get Rogue buffs. I went for the points with this one. I figure we need every edge we can get."

"Right." Horc nodded. He hadn't been thinking about racial buffs and things like that when he'd rolled up his character. He'd let everything but the name be random. He hadn't planned on playing Halfworld longer than necessary to get the bonus money from work for beta testing. He defiantly hadn't planned on getting stuck in the game. Also, he hadn't expected to enjoy the game the way he was. Even if he still hadn't admitted it to any of his friends, the game had grown on him and he planned on continuing to play, once they got the problems with the AI sorted out and it was safe again. He wanted to be like all the other players and not have to worry about if he was ever going to escape the game and be able to live his normal life again.

The door opened and Bo' stuck his head in. "Hey Yous Guys, it's time for the next round." He paused and his large eyes got even bigger. "Wait a minute, did yous' Rogue become a Fighter?"

Horc got off the bed and shrugged. "I guess you could say that. We're still a party of three."

Bo' frowned. "And only two of yous are the original party."

"But there wasn't anything about that in the paperwork Greensleeves signed, was there?"

"No." Bo' looked thoughtful, then shook his head hard enough that his long green ears flopped against his nose. "I guess there isn't. It does change up the dynamics of the fight though."

Honestly, Horc didn't care how much it changed up the dynamics of the fight. If Rothand had things figured out based on a party's classes, then he might be in for a surprise. As long as they weren't dealing with three people who could turn invisible, except to other invisible players, he didn't think it was going to be a major problem, for them at least.

THE NEXT group they fought in the arena was Greensleeves, Stanishollyshmite, and an Ursan Ranger named Ted who had a huge black bear at his side. Horc swallowed hard. He knew Tufkakes had enough time to get through and let Greensleeves know the plan, but that didn't help the tightening in his gut about facing a partymate, and good friend, in the arena. The very thought of it made the games seem that much crueller.

"Great, two with healing abilities," Titanya said. "Let's hope Tufkakes got through to them. Maybe he even told Stanishollyshmite" She pulled her huge sword as the opposite gate slammed shut.

"He might've told Stan?" Baladara asked in a soft hiss. "Why would he tell Stan?"

Titanya looked confused. "I thought he was supposed to let everyone know. It makes sense."

Baladara shook her head. "Yeah, but Stan? I bet he told the other two too. We really could've left them here for a while and let them figure it out for themselves."

"That wouldn't have been nice," Horc said. He wasn't exactly fond of the mailroom morons either, but they didn't deserve to suffer any more than anyone else did.

"We don't have time to debate this." Titanya charged as Ted unleashed his first round of arrows. She headed toward the Ranger.

As one of the three projectiles came at him, Horc dodged out of the way and rolled on the sand, coming up to release a Fire arrow at the other ranger.

Baladara got off a spell and Ted's next barrage hit an invisible barrier in front of them.

"Isn't that a little odd to you," Baladara muttered as her hands began to glow red as she prepped a fireball. "I mean, almost like enslaving a cousin."

Horc couldn't bring himself to fire on Greensleeves, even as the Druid's hands glowed brown and the first tendrils of a sandstorm swirled toward them. "Oh, you mean an Ursan having a bear companion?"

Wolf charged into the fight, engaging the much larger companion animal. The sight made Horc wince and he hoped his wolf would be okay. With Titanya helping him, he had a chance.

"Yeah." Baladara got off her spell and a Fireball caught Stanishollyshmite in the chest as the Paladin rushed toward them.

"Maybe he's looking out for a cousin." Horc sent a Poison arrow at the bear, even as the Ursan shouldered his bow, pulled out a huge axe and charged toward them.

"Could be." Baladara got off a round of Magical Force Bolts that damaged Stanishollyshmite, but not a lot.

The force of the sandstorm hit Baladara's shield. Dust collected on the magical barrier and blocked out their view across the arena.

"Damn." Baladara rubbed her head. "That one's got feedback with it."

Horc got off another Flame arrow as Ted lumbered closer. "What do you mean feedback?"

"Magical feedback from the force of two or more magical…" Baladara shook her head. "Remind me when we're done here to explain it to you."

The wind abruptly dropped and the dust fell back to the sand. Horc caught a glimpse of Tufkakes stepping away from Greensleeves as the Druid dropped to the sand. He started to shout an objection, but Ted hit Baladara's magical shield at the same time the Paladin did.

"Coming down." Baladara muttered.

Horc fired one last arrow at the bear that Wolf and Titanya were still fighting. He spared a glance at their health bars. They were close, but Wolf had slightly more than the bear. With luck, it would be enough. Titanya looked like she was holding out pretty well.

Jumping back from Ted's first swing, Horc dropped his bow and pulled his sword. He managed to get it out in time to block Ted's next attack. The impact shook Horc, and he nearly dropped the sword as he struggled to maintain a good grip on the pommel. He was forced back by the sheer force of the Ursan's strength. It was more than he'd expected.

"You've been doing well, Half Orc," Ted said. "But I've been doing better. If we win enough fights, they say we'll get to log out."

"Don't count on that," Horc snapped as he swung his blade up to come in a little higher on the Ursan. His problem was, even though his toon was larger, compared to Elves and Humans, the Ursan had several inches on him, and a good fifty to seventy-five pounds. It was an uneven fight, even if they were the same class and within a couple of levels of each other.

"Steelmaiden was a mighty fighter." Ted swung his ax again, forcing Horc to dodge out of the way. "She won many fights and is no longer with us. She must've been allowed to log out."

From what he was saying, Horc realized Tufkakes hadn't had time to get to everyone. He glanced around the arena, trying not to take his eyes off Ted too long. There was no sign of Tufkakes. The Rogue must've disappeared back into the shadows.

Horc shook his head. "She got out another way." He smashed his sword hard and fast at Ted, scoring a critical hit to Ted's ax arm and dropping his health by three eighths.

Ted staggered back under Horc's blows, switching his weapon to his other hand and trying to block Horc's attacks.

"Be ready to log out when you die." Horc said as he body slammed Ted, pressing Ted's good hand and weapon against his chest. He kneed Ted hard in the groin, not knowing if that even worked in the game, or against an Ursan. Then as Ted wobbled back a couple of steps, he swung his sword as hard as he could at Ted's head.

He scored another critical hit, managing to decapitate the other Ranger.

In the distance, a bear roared.

Horc spun and reached for his bow even as he remembered he'd dropped it when Ted had hit Baladara's magical shield. Ted's bear was ignoring Wolf and Titanya's attacks and charging toward him.

Spreading his legs to give himself a better base, Horc held his sword at the ready. He was only going to get one hit in before the bear plowed into him, driven into a fury at the death of his Ranger. The bear was down to under a quarter health. Even as it charged, Wolf and Titanya were scoring hits on it. Its health bar was down into the orange as Horc took his swing.

He held his breath as his blade swung down toward the black shaggy head. Somehow, he missed. The bear slammed into him, driving him to the arena sand. Its teeth clamped down on his shoulder, sending pain through his body.

No sooner had its weight hit him and the agony went through him, and it was gone.

Horc blinked.

The bear lay on its side next to him. Its health bar disappeared and it started to pixelate and vanish.

"Okay, Dude, if you weren't so attached to Wolf, I'd say ditch him and get yourself a bear." Baladara shook out her hands. "That bugger was hard to take down."

Titanya nodded and stopped down to wipe her blade off in the sand. "I have to agree. I take it you dealt with the Paladin."

"Fairly easy if you know Stan's weak spots." Baladara grinned

"But yous guys cheated." Bo' came out of the tunnel that led back to the combatants sleeping chambers. The goblin looked furious.

"What do you mean?" Horc asked, spreading his hands, trying to look innocent. Then it hit him what was going on.

"Yous brought four men to a three-man fight." Bo' bounced a small, nasty looking club in his hand. "That means you're all disqualified."

Behind Bo' several more pirates appeared out of the tunnel. They all had weapons out and looked pissed off.

23

HORC'S HEART sank. He glanced at his health bar, it was under half. Titanya's, Baladara's were low too. Tufkakes was the only one with over three quarters. They weren't up for taking on several fighters at or above their level. It wasn't going to be a fair fight. He'd feel really stupid if he died both in game and IRL because the rapidly learning AI was trying to use players as its personal toys.

"Drink this." Baladara tossed a vial at Horc. Two more went flying toward the others.

Faster than he could've managed in the real world, Horc snatched the glass tube out of midair, uncorked it, and drank it. His health bar flashed and was back to full. He dropped the bottle in his bag as he whipped out a chunk of meat and hurled it toward Wolf.

Horc had just enough time to bring his sword up in an attempt to block Bo's club. After fighting Ted, the Ursan, switching to a foe who was barely up to his stomach felt awkward, and Bo's fist blow made Horc stumble backward a couple of steps.

"I'd thought yous guys was up to something," Bo' screeched as he swung the club at Horc again. "But the boss said yous was just good fighters. Now yous's going to be able to fight for us."

"Back down, Bo'," Horc pleaded. The NPC wasn't part of his party, but after all their interactions, he felt like Bo' might've been a friend in another reality. There was something about him that reminded Horc of one of the guys he'd worked with a couple of years earlier who moved from New Jersey to Texas when the sea levels had risen to the point that the coastal towns had flooded and the hurricanes had come so frequently he'd had to leave. "We don't want to hurt anyone, we just want to get out of the arena and go on with our adventuring."

Bo' rolled and dodged away from Horc's attack. "Too bad, yous ain't going nowhere." He sprang to his feet and rushed Horc.

"I don't know what happens to NPCs when you die—" Horc blocked another attack, this time not losing any ground to Bo' "—but you're going to find out." He wanted to make Bo's death quick and as painless as possible. If NPCs felt pain.

With Bo's club sliding along the edge of Horc's sword, Horc swung up and forced Bo' to stumble. Wolf was there in an instant and hit Bo' hard in the chest, carrying the diminutive Goblin to the ground.

Bo' screamed as his club hit the ground and rolled out of his grasp. He grabbed fists-full of fur and tried to head-butt Wolf.

As Horc went to help Wolf finish off the Goblin, one of the other Pirates, a huge Ogre with massive shoulders and an off-white bald head that made him look undead, swung a huge pike at Horc. The metal tip of the pike clanged off Horc's sword as he brought the weapon around to barely block the blow. Again, he was forced back as Bo' continued to scream like the sound was going to defend him from Wolf.

"We need you to die," the Ogre shouted as he swung the pike at Horc again.

Not exactly sure how he managed to do it, Horc brought his sword down to stop the nasty blade again. As he took another step back from the force of the blow, Horc knew he had to change the tide quickly. From his display, he could tell the Ogre was the same level he was, but was more than twice his size, and had a much longer reach. Constantly having to change the type of opponents he was fighting confused Horc. He needed some consistency.

"In case you haven't noticed," Horc caught the massive pike again, this time on the wooden shaft. "We don't die easily."

"He's got that right," Tufkakes stepped out of the shadows behind the Ogre and drove a blade into its unprotected neck.

Nearly half of the Ogre's health vanished from the blow.

The Ogre reached back as if to swat at Tufkakes, but he was already gone, disappearing back into the shadows.

Horc took advantage of the Ogre being distracted and rammed the tip of his sword into the big Pirate's gut and yanked upwards. The smell that rushed out was reminiscent of spoiled fish patties and made Horc gag as the Ogre bellowed and fell back, yanking Horc's sword out of his hands.

A critical hit notification flashed on the screen and the Ogre stopped moving.

"You killed Slag!" Another large pirate shouted and rushed away from Titanya, swinging his massive sword at Horc.

As he went to bring his sword up to block the blow, Horc realized his hands were empty and his sword was in the Ogre, presumably Slag. He ducked under the new attacker's swing and punched the big guy as hard as he could in the nuts.

"Don't run away from me." Titanya's next blow caught the Ogre hard in the back, spraying blood in a bright arc that splashed all three of them.

Horc got his hands around his sword and yanked it free of Slag's body just as the carcass started to digitize and fade away. He wasn't sure if he'd have lost the sword if it had still been in the corpse when that happened.

THE ARENA

The big Human Pirate grabbed Horc's shoulder and yanked him around. His face was still a wash of pain from the attacks he'd suffered. "You're toast, Ranger."

"Not right now." Horc swung up as hard as he could. He didn't have time to aim the blow, and it skimmed along the Pirate's shin and up through his arm.

Titanya managed to get another excellent slash on his back and the Pirate collapsed to the ground, dead.

"You need healing," Titanya said as she turned to where the other pirates were going down quickly.

Horc glanced at his health bar that was flashing in the orange. He was close to dying. One more good hit and he was done for. Around the arena, the crowds were cheering.

"We don't have a healer right now," Horc said, wishing he had a supply of healing potions in his bag. If he survived the arena, he was going to make sure he never left home without them again.

"Then we might be in for a problem." Titanya frowned and glanced to where Tufkakes and Baladara were fighting the last two Pirates.

"No!" Bo' screamed, then went silent.

Wolf shook his head, as if he was trying to get the taste of Goblin out of his mouth. From the party icons showing on the right side of Horc's vision, Wolf was fairly low on health too, but it was something he could help with. He reached in his bag and pulled out a chunk of meat.

"Eat it before following us." Horc tossed the meat to his companion. He looked at Titanya. "Let's finish this."

The Warrior woman grinned and nodded. Her health was about half down. "Let's." She charged the Dwarven Pirate Tufkakes had down to almost a quarter.

Horc glanced over to where he'd dropped his bow earlier. It would've been smart to shoot the Human Pirate Baladara was struggling with, but it would've taken more time than just running across the sand and stabbing it in the back.

Moving as fast and quietly as he could, Horc hoped between the roar of the crowd and Baladara's repeated short sword swings, the Pirate wouldn't know he was coming. He didn't have Tufkakes' Shadow Walking ability, or Backstab attack, but it didn't matter. Baladara's manna was gone and her health was nearly there too. Horc wasn't under any illusion that if any of them died in the arena, the AI would do its best to keep them prisoners. Even if his health was low, he had to do what he could to save his friends.

Horc managed to drive his sword deep into the Pirate's back.

"Shit!" the Pirate shouted and swung around fast. He jerked the sword out of Horc's hands and managed to land a meaty punch to Horc's jaw.

As the critical hit to the Pirate flashed in Horc's view, his own health flashed red. Horc stumbled backward. His head throbbed, and he tried to get some kind of focus. In the distance he heard his party mates shouting. He wondered if he was done for. He fought to figure out what was happening, but his vision swam and he crashed to the sand, getting a mouthful of grit and dirt.

He lay there, his health bar flashing red and a low health warning scrolling every few seconds through his vision. The next hit wasn't even going to need to be a solid hit and he'd go down and stay that way. He'd pushed things too far and lost. It was over. He just hoped the rescue team had his pod stabilized and he wasn't going to die for real, but even if he did, at least he was going to die saving a friend. That was a good thing.

Something, or someone hit the sand beside him, sending up a cloud of dust that then rained down on him.

A huge hand grabbed Horc's neck and lifted him from the sand. The smell of rotting vegetation washed over him, making him gag. Horc forced his eyes opened and stared into the angry face of Rothand, the Pirate lord of the arena. His beady red eyes were squinted in anger and his other fist was drawn back to punch Horc hard in the face.

Horc had no doubt that Rothand's ruggedly ugly visage with its massive tusks was going to be the last thing he ever saw.

24

"YOU'RE A lot of trouble, Ranger." Rothand's breath was hot on Horc's face. "You'll make a good addition to my stable of fighters."

Determined to not just go down without fighting, Horc kicked Rothand as hard as he could in the groin.

Rothand's fist began its journey toward Horc's nose.

Magic tingled around Horc. It was a familiar feeling. His health bar stopped flashing red as Rothand's fist landed with a solid crack, sending him back into the red.

"What?" Rothand went to hit Horc again, but a Fireball engulfed the half-breed Pirate.

The healing magic hit Horc again. He kicked Rothand again, then the Pirate huffed and stumbled like something had just caught him from behind.

"Drop him and face me!" Titanya roared. "Let me show you what a woman can do to you when you're not controlling her."

As Horc's health jumped up to half, Rothand let go of his neck and he fell to the sandy arena surface. The swamp-like reek of the Pirate's hand vanished. Horc's health dropped back down, but not all the way into the red.

"Anytime." Rothand turned from Horc and got a face full of angry Wolf before he could take two steps.

The Half-Orc Pirate stumbled and Horc rolled to grab him around the knees. The combined attack brought the man down hard, just as another Fireball went sailing over the three of them.

"Don't help him dodge my attack," Baladara shouted. "I don't have full mana here."

Horc wished he had a sword, an axe…something. He didn't think he'd be able to do much against a foe, particularly one with three stars next to his name that had so many levels on him.

His quiver caught him in the back, reminding him that even if he had dropped his bow, he still had his arrows. He grabbed one, it was better than nothing, and jabbed it into Rothand's thigh as hard as he could. The Pirate screamed, although the attack didn't appear to do much to his health bar.

Titanya hit him hard in the head with her huge sword. From the way his health dropped a noticeable amount, Horc figured she'd managed a critical hit, but it wasn't enough to even drop him by a quarter of this health.

A heavy, furry hand pulled Horc away from the fight. "You'd better step back a bit."

Someone handed him his bow. "You might need this."

Horc took the bow and stared at the two new players. **Bigdaddybear, Ursan, Druid, Level 35,** brushed dust from Horc's shoulder.

Stanoran, Human, Priest, Level 35 pulled out his massive silver mace.

"We've got more people coming in if we need them," Bigdaddybear said with a lilt in his voice that sounded a lot like Greensleeves.

Horc gapped at them. "David?"

Bigdaddybear nodded. "This was Rick's idea." He gestured down his body.

"We don't have time to talk," Stanoran said. "Even with us, this isn't going to be an easy fight."

"Point." Bigdaddybear grinned. "Good thing the Ursans have a higher constitution than Humans or

Elves." His hands glowed a dark green as he started casting a spell. "Gotta knock this fool down."

Horc drew back an arrow and added Poison to it. "Let's do this."

Between Tufkakes, Baladara, and Titanya they had Rothand down to nearly half, but they were all hurting too. Rothand had pulled out his wickedly curved blade and was doing a good job keeping the others at bay, as they tried to close in on him to do more damage.

Each arrow Horc hit the Pirate with didn't seem to do any real damage to him, but the damage over time of the Poison arrows did seem to start gnawing at his health while the others hit him with all they had.

Staying back from the hand to hand fighting, Horc kept firing arrows with spells on them to augment their damage for as long as his mana held out. As his mana bar went out, he reached back for an arrow and realized his quiver was empty too.

Rothand was down to three eighths health or so. But the others weren't faring well. Stanoran had fallen back and was constantly casting healing spells on the others to keep them going, but his mana was starting to drop quickly.

Bigdaddybear slipped behind Rothand and picked him up in a massive bear hug.

Rothand hacked at Bigdaddybear's arms, but it seemed to be to no avail.

Titanya slashed at Rothand, seeming to aim for his neck, but the Pirate twisted in the Ursan's hold, and her blow landed on his shoulder. Even still, it was enough to knock a decent chunk out of his health as a Fireball hit him in the face from the other side.

He was down to a quarter health.

Horc looked around for his sword and couldn't see it anywhere.

Wolf was at Baladara's side but was down into the red himself.

There was nothing in the arena Horc could use as a weapon. Then an idea hit him; he ran to where Tufkakes was stepping out of the shadows, driving a dagger into Rothand's neck. The Pirate jerked at just the right moment, and the blow landed on his collarbone, not doing a lot of damage.

"Tufkakes, loan me a dagger." Horc held out his hand. "We can hit him together."

"That might help." Tufkakes pulled a dagger from somewhere and tossed it to Horc.

Again, catching it more agilely than he would've been able to do IRL, Horc felt better with a blade in his hand.

"Hurry Guys, I can't keep him up like this." Bigdaddybear's waist was bent backwards, trying to keep the Pirate off the ground.

With a deep breath, Horc focused on the side of Rothand's shaggy head, hoping he was aiming for the ear like he thought he was. He drove the blade deep at the same time Tufkakes did.

Rothand twisted as if to avoid the blows but rolled his head so Horc's blade slid into his red eye. The Pirate Lord roared in agony, then went limp in Bigdaddybear's hands.

Horc let out a long slow breath or relief as Bigdaddybear tossed Rothand's body to the side. Around them, the people in the stands had gone eerily silent.

Tufkakes rushed to loot the body. After a second he stood with his hands on his hips. "What is this? He doesn't have any loot. How does the boss not have any loot?"

Baladara brushed dust off her robes. "Not only that, but we didn't get any XP for that."

Horc brought up his quest window. The quest to vanquish the darkness was still there. "I've still got the quest too. If Rothand wasn't the darkness, then who, or what is?"

Something rumbled deep under the arena. The ground shifted. Rothand pixelated and vanished as the sand covered his body, then flattened out.

"Health potions!" Horc shouted. They were all down and not in any shape to take on anything else at that moment. Even Bigdaddybear and Stanoran were down some points and they were both low on mana and wouldn't be able to heal them that much more. Just when it looked like they were finished, something else was going to come at them.

Horc was starting to hate fantasy games again.

25

PEOPLE IN the stands screamed as Horc rushed over to Baladara. "Seriously, break out the health potions."

Baladara shook her head. "Sorry. All out. This trip has been expensive in terms of potions."

The ground shook again.

"Not a good time." Horc paused as magic danced across his skin. He glanced over and both Bigdaddybear and Stanoran were casting spells. The glow of healing magic covered their hands.

"Guys, was that smart?" Horc felt a little better at having his health back to full, but he didn't like the idea of their healers being low on manna.

"Only option," Bigdaddybear replied as he reached into his bag and pulled out two potions. "Besides we've got…"

The shaking got worse, and then the sand of the arena exploded up and out.

Horc flew through the air, landing hard on one of the concrete benches that filled the stands. He'd somehow managed to not hit any of the other players on his way to his impact site. He lay there for a moment as deep laughing filled the sky.

He opened his eyes and a huge Red Dragon filled the sky above the arena. In its talons it carried a cage with several captives in it. Slasher was pressed against the metal bars.

"You're not taking the system down!" The Dragon continued to hover above them. "It's my system now. You can't turn things off without killing these people."

Horc wished he wasn't out of arrows. Around him, players cast Fireballs, Lighting Bolts, and other distance spells. They all bounced off the Dragon's hide and didn't seem to faze it in the least. The text above the Dragon read **Pyranous, Red Dragon, Level XXX** there were also four stars after its name.

Horc swallowed hard. There was no way for them to take on such a foe. It was the most powerful mob they'd seen in the game.

With another laugh, Pyranous stopped hovering, leveled out and flew off across the ocean, the cage still grasped in his talons.

"What are we going to do now?" Horc asked as he tried to make sense of what he'd just seen. Pyranous had to be the body the AI had constructed for itself, although why it had an identifier when the programmers who appeared in the game didn't, didn't make any sense to him. If the AI was so powerful, it shouldn't be any different from them, unless it was still learning what it was capable of.

"We follow it, of course," Titanya said. "I really wish I could be Steelmaiden again. I like Barbarians better, even if she had picked up bugs."

"Let's talk to Rick about it." Bigdaddybear sighed and sat on the side of the wall, facing Horc. The thick stonewall was cracked and looked ready to crumble at any moment.

"You do that. I'll see about rounding up more players." Tufkakes looked around. "Okay, is it just me, or did most of the other players just vanish?"

"Looks like folks are finally wising up in the game and getting out," Bigdaddybear said. "Rick says population just dropped and people are continuing to log out."

"About time," Horc said, feeling a little better about people disappearing. If they were logging out they were safe from the AI… Pyranous. "What about the rest of us?"

"Rick's checking the servers, seeing if he can find a way to isolate things."

"Ask him about our XP," Baladara said, plopping down next to Horc. "I just checked mine and we haven't gotten anything since our last fight in the arena. We should've gotten points for Bo' and his menacing mateys."

Bigdaddybear nodded. "Working on it."

Another Ursan appeared in the stands near them. His text read **Theodore, Ursan, Shaman, Level 35.**

"Theodore?" Baladara said. "Don't tell me, you used to be Ted."

Theodore nodded. "I'm not that great with character names. Sorry I was late, it took a little work to get a character I liked."

"We needed people hitting things," Baladara snapped. "I don't think at this point it matters if you like the toon or not."

"Rick's going to have to work on why the XP system stopped working for us," Bigdaddybear said.

"XP stopped working, what happened?" Theodore asked with a frown.

"We're not sure," Horc said. A strange energy buzzed through him, it felt like he was being torn apart. "Something's happening here." He went to step back away from his friends but caught his calf on the seat behind him. He stumbled back and an odd void opened up around him, pulling him away from the arena and his friends. Somewhere in the distance, Wolf howled and Horc's world went black.

ALAN BLINKED and stared at the familiar pod lid above him. There were lights above him brighter than they should've been. He tapped the controls that should bring up his game selection display, but nothing was responding. He lifted hands that felt like lead and weakly tapped on the window. "Send me back!"

Horc's adventure continues in "Beyond the Boss"

If you'd like to stay on top of new releases and upcoming
work by Drew Seren, please join our mailing list.
And if you enjoyed Horc's adventure, please leave a
review. It's easy and won't take you very long.

Drew Seren Bio

Drew Seren was raised on a diet of science fiction, both in print and on the screen. He spent many nights watching Star Trek and Space 1999 with his father. Comic books were a main staple of his reading, and then when he was in high school he started reading *Dragon Riders of Pern* and quickly began devouring any science fiction he could, luckily his father had an extensive library at the time. He started writing soon after that, letting writing help him make it through class. During college and his corporate life, Drew spent a lot of time writing to help him endure the mundane things that gnawed at him. Through his twenties and thirties, comic books and science fiction helped him survive. To this day, he's still reading as much or more than he's writing. He's also an avid gamer, playing first *Dungeons and Dragons*, and currently lots of *World of Warcraft*. He's recently turned his attention to writing full time and exploring the vast galaxy through new and interesting eyes.

Stay in touch with Drew through his website
www.drewseren.com

and Facebook pages
fb.me/drewseren

Feel free to drop me an email
drew@drewseren.com